Flaming Canyon

Flaming Canyon

WALKER A. TOMPKINS

Sagebrush
Large Print Westerns

Library of Congress Cataloging in Publication Data

Tompkins, Walker A.
     Flaming canyon / Walker A. Tompkins.
        p.   cm.
     ISBN 1-57490-091-9 (alk. paper)
     1. Large type books. I. Title.
[PS3539. O3897F57   1997]
813'.54--dc21   97-24395
                                                                                        CIP

Cataloguing in Publication Data is available from
the British Library and the National Library of Australia.

Sagebrush Large Print Westerns are published in the United States
and Canada by Thomas T. Beeler, Publisher, Box 659, Hampton
Falls, New Hampshire 03844-0659. ISBN 1-57490-091-9

Published in the United Kingdom, Eire, and the Republic of South
Africa by Isis Publishing Ltd, 7 Centremead, Osney Mead, Oxford
OX2 0ES England. ISBN 0-7531-5594-X

Published in Australia and New Zealand by Australian Large Print
Audio & Video Pty Ltd, 17 Mohr Street, Tullamarine, Victoria, 3043,
Australia. ISBN 1-86340-736-7

Manufactured in the United States of America

For Frank, Hallie And Jay
remembering Windemere and Wilsonian.

The locale of this novel actually exists and the principal events of the plot—the fire and flood which spelled the doom of Conconully, for instance—are historical facts. *Flaming Canyon* and the characters herein are wholly fictional.

CHAPTER ONE

SHOWDOWN AT THE FERRY

THE TANDEM-HITCHED CONESTOGAS CARAVANED IN majestic silhouette against the darkening sky, sway-backed canvas hoods catching the red glare of sunset before they dipped into blue shadow beneath the flat rim of the scab-rock plateau.

At the foot of the cliffs where the lights of the Port Columbia stage depot bloomed in the twilight, the Brewster ferry was tied up at its slip. Three passengers waiting for the Yakima stage to pull out stood by the ferry tender watching the wagons crawl down the switchbacks toward the river.

Ed Guerrant, the ferryman, spoke softly from the deck. "That's Del Troy coming now, Mr. Herrod. Hauling minin' machinery from Spokane to the Okanogan diggin's upriver. He always crosses the Columbia here."

The passenger addressed as Herrod spoke around the unlighted cigar in his teeth. "Who'll be driving the second string?"

"Most likely that albino partner who followed Troy out from Texas," Guerrant said. "Feller name of Whitey Crade."

Herrod gestured at Guerrant without turning to face him. "Take the ferry across and tie up. I'll handle Troy."

A girl standing a short distance away watched the ferry move out into the river, straining at its parallel cables. Doc Godette stood beside Herrod, a scrawny figure in his Confederate gray coat, an ancient brass

1

telescope screwed to his eye, its lenses focused on the oncoming wagons.

Midway out on the ferry slip pilings, Fred Bolte checked the wick of his unlighted lantern and watched the fishline he had in the water. There was a certain tenseness in Bolte which seemed to be shared by the girl.

"I hope you know what you're doing, Bix," the girl spoke through the dusk. "This man Troy will be desperate when he learns what you have done. You know he's racing against time to get those wagons to Conconully."

Bix Herrod regarded the girl with an obscure amusement. "If Troy stands in our way, he must step aside—or be forced aside. That's up to him, Shasta."

The girl moved away from the ferry landing, as if dreading the showdown she knew would soon transpire there, and walked up the slope to where a hostler was hitching a fresh span of Morgans to the waiting Concord.

Troy's wagons were at the foot of the talus slope now, rumbling down the Port Columbia road toward the ferry landing. Bix Herrod loosened the cross-draw revolvers in their holsters at his flanks, and flexed his finger muscles like a pugilist readying himself for battle.

"Troy wears no guns," Doc Godette reported, telescoping his spyglass and tucking it under an arm. "You'll bait him into no shooting tonight, Bix."

A certain disappointment touched Herrod as he pondered Godette's report. Finally he shrugged and started upslope to the stage stand, the oldster following him.

Guerrant's ferryboat was lost in the dark reflections of the foothills looming above the west bank of the river. Fred Bolte, knowing his role in the drama to come, reeled in his fishline and made another cast. The stage was set for trouble tonight. There was no way of knowing how Del Troy would meet it.

As the wagons drew closer to the stage depot, details drew into sharper definition. Each of the jerkline mule teams was driven by a man who rode a saddled nigh-wheeler, and the stamp of a grueling desert crossing lay on wagons and mules and drivers alike. Columbia Basin alkali had neutralized the canvas-hooded wagons and the flesh and clothing of Del Troy and his partner with an over-all drab hue.

Punishing late-June heat and dried-up waterholes and recurrent breakdowns of overloaded wagons had plagued the freighters on this trek. But the urgency of meeting a contract deadline and the disaster which its expiration would bring to their personal fortunes had driven the men, kept them in the saddle beyond the normal limits of their endurance.

Now the hellish nightmare was behind them. Red sunset—the fifth to overtake them out of Spokane—smoldered beyond the looming granite teeth of the Cascades in a burned-out cauldron glow as the gaunted mules followed the down-grade toward the welcome coolness of greening bottomland.

The sweet promise of water, the first since their torturous by-passage of Grand Coulee's whelming barrier, reached the ears and nostrils of men and animals, quickening their progress toward the ferry landing. Beyond the Columbia's whispering breadth lay the Okanogan country and trail's end.

Unaware of the appraising eyes upon him, Troy rode at a hipshot slouch in the saddle, a sun-blackened Texan of thirty-odd whose hands coiled slack on jerkline, taut

3

on brake rope. His body juices were drained dry by the desert crossing, his nerves at the raw fringe of breaking for want of food and rest.

But tomorrow's dawn marked the due-date for delivering this emergency freight in Ruby and Conconully. Only the river remained as a barrier to be breached.

Under the dust-veneered sag of his Stetson brim, Troy's smoky, raw-red eyes swept the welcome vista of purple footslopes lifting beyond the Columbia River in receding corrugated waves to meet the cerise ribbon of the lofty skyline.

Lights twinkled in a crosshatched pattern on the far bank, civilization outposted by the deadfalls and honkies of Brewster. Closer at hand, the lamps of the Port Columbia stagecoach stand threw their fanwise yellow glow on a waiting Concord, silhouetting the man and the girl who watched the wagons rumble by.

Chain tugs clanked and stretchers and lead bars made metallic discord in the dusk's hush as Troy halted his mules at the foot of the ferry ramp. The ferry, he noted, was tied up on the west bank tonight, which meant a vexing delay at a time when every hour was precious to him.

He stepped down from stirrups with the stilted awkwardness of a man made bone-weary by eighteen hours under the debilitating sun of the Washington plateau. Behind the lead wagon with its trailer and canvas-tarped caboose, Whitey Crade halted his mules and dismounted, eyeing the Port Columbia saloon with a sullen thirst nagging his vitals. Crade knew the futility of suggesting an overnight stop here. Whisky and sleep must wait until this freight was discharged and the waybills signed by Steen Slankard.

4

Crade felt a peevish impatience needle him as he watched Troy flank his lathered team, pausing solicitously to ease a swingspanner's galled collar, move on to rub a leader's gaskin with a handful of green weeds.

Finally Troy crossed over to the hoof-splintered ramp of the ferry landing and yanked the clapper rope of the iron bell on its standard, to signal the ferryman on the opposite bank that a payload was waiting for service.

When the anvil tones of the ferry tender's answering bell volleyed back from the Brewster side, Troy removed his Stetson and swatted the dust from his hickory shirt and shotgun chaps.

The sudden glare of a lantern startled him, drawing his eye to a lone cowpuncher who was fishing for sockeye salmon out on the splintered pilings of the ferry slip. Across a gap of time and distance Troy believed he had seen this cowhand with the fishhooks adorning the band of his black sombrero. He had a mental picture of this man fishing for cats in the Pecos, and he tarried to confirm the hunch.

"You're Fred Bolte, ain't you? Used to ride bodyguard for Bix Herrod on the Chisholm Trail?"

The fisherman lifted his lantern to put its yellow shine on the speaker. Beaver teeth glinted under his ram's horn mustache. "Well, Troy. Small world. Didn't know you'd come West."

Troy watched Bolte haul in his line to land a forty-pounder. "Some difference between that Chinook and a Nueces bullhead, eh, Bolte? Everything is bigger out here."

Bolte said, "You knew Bix Herrod, eh? He's up at the stage yonder with Doc Godette. You know Doc? Always travel together."

Troy considered this information for a moment, not liking it. "I saw a girl as I passed. She with them?"

Bolte took out a knife and slit his fish from end to end. "Shasta Ives. Owns the Dollar outfit down Yakima way."

"Colonel Sam's daughter. I've heard of her."

Bolte sensed that the lean Texan was not making idle conversation, so he amplified his remark. "Old Sam died last winter. Bix and Shasta aimed to get married this fall."

"I heard about that, too," Troy said, and moved back to his wagons. Whitey Crade was seated astraddle the bullbar plank which jutted behind his lead wagon, and the glow of the stage lanterns revealed the sullen cast of the albino's milk-white features. Troy hunkered down beside his partner, building a smoke and letting the tension ease from his overtaxed muscles.

"Shouldn't have let you auger me into leavin' the Brazos," Crade grumbled, airing a chronic grouse. "Mulewhackin' ain't my game. Are we supposed to be ranchers or slaves to a jerkline string? I tell you, Del, I'm getting a bellyful of this."

Bix Herrod and another man left the girl at the stage door and angled down the slope toward the freight caravan. The ennui in Troy's throbbing eyes gave way to a sharpening interest as he watched them approach, wondering what had brought the Yakima cattleman this far north; and apprehension touched him briefly as he pulled his thoughts back to Whitey Crade's complaint.

"Like I've told you for two years now," Troy said wearily, having been over this many times before, "we've got a range and no stock. If hauling freight for Slankard & Company will make the money we need to build up a herd, these hauls are worth the grief they cost us."

6

Bix Herrod halted before them, appraising the crated machinery under the Conestoga hoods. He was a big man, this Herrod, bigger than Troy remembered him being, back in Texas; perhaps because he carried himself with the unconscious swagger that went with the ownership of Washington's biggest cattle outfit.

He wore his Keevil hat and tailor-made fustian and Hussar boots as a king might wear crown and purple robe, and a touch of that arrogance flavored the man's greeting as he turned back to Troy.

"Didn't expect our trails would cross out here, Del."

Troy nodded, his attention shifting to Herrod's companion. Doc Godette was a rawboned oldster, doubled up at the moment in a paroxysm of spongy coughs which betokened the last stages of consumption. The old medico's face was whisky-bloated and along his caved-in cheek lay the scar of a Yankee saber, scribbling its puckered whiteness from temple to jaw. Doc Godette had aged in the years since Troy had seen him in Abilene.

"Howdy, Godette. Bolte tells me you're getting married, Bix. Congratulations."

The coal on the end of Herrod's cheroot ebbed and glowed, illuminating the rigid planes of a darkly handsome face and the close-clipped mustache which was italicized by the line of a wide and predatory mouth.

"Thanks. Shasta and I have been checking on summer range up in the Okanogans this past week."

Troy lit his cigarette, a premonition of trouble building up in him. Instinct told him that Herrod had engineered this seemingly chance meeting at Port Columbia tonight.

"I heard the drought hit Yakima and Ellensburg range

7

pretty hard this summer," he agreed banally. "Graze is good between here and the Canadian border."

Herrod's eyes focused on Troy with a calculating intensity. "Shasta and I aim to summer our beef in Flaming Canyon," he said through a burst of fragrant cigar smoke. "I used the Canyon three years ago when the winter die-up whittled down my Lazy H feeders. It's comforting to know there's government graze available to tide us over."

Del Troy's sloping hat brim hid the sudden harsh fixture of his mouth as he pondered this disclosure of Herrod's plans. Doc Godette walked over to the landing-slip where Bolte was, as if he sensed heavy weather in the offing.

"Reckon I got bad news for you, Bix," Troy commented. "Whitey Crade and I have proved up on adjoining homesteads at the mouth of Flaming Canyon. Aim to stock our range this fall and build up a herd of our own."

For a moment the silence was broken only by Whitey Crade's accelerated breathing, betraying his concern over what lay just ahead.

"Yeah?" Herrod echoed. "I heard a couple of small-tally squatters had fenced off the Canyon entrance this spring. I'm glad to hear it's a fellow Texan I got to deal with. Don't reckon you'll object to Dollar and Lazy H shoving a trail herd across your land to reach the upper Canyon?"

Troy dropped his cigarette stub and ground it out underheel, thinking, *This is what Bix has been leading up to tonight.*

"Sorry, Herrod. But I took a year's lease on the whole length of Flaming Canyon this spring. From Okanogan Jones, the squaw man who owns most of the range in the Twenty-Mile Strip between our homesteads and the Canadian line. I've got haying crews harvesting the graze starting this week. Aim to use it for winter feed."

Herrod's cigar glowed brighter under the hard pull of his lips. "Implying that I can hunt elsewhere for summer range?"

Troy nodded, his eyes bleak in the darkness. "Stacks up that way, Bix. Canyon grass belongs to me and the nesters who are cutting and stacking it on shares."

Herrod hunkered down to Troy's level, and his voice came now in a sharp, imperative undertone. "I'll lay my cards on the table, Troy. Our herd is already on the trail from Yakima. I expect to shove my beef into Flaming Canyon early next week. I don't propose to let any drift fence stop me."

Troy absorbed the impact of Herrod's flat ultimatum in silence. He had a clear picture of how things stood between them now. Herrod's beef was moving north, headed for the lush graze which made Flaming Canyon the choicest range in northern Washington. Herrod was warning him to move out or face a showdown.

"Listen," Troy said carefully, measuring his words. "Flaming Canyon is closed this summer. When your steers show up next week, keep them clear of our fence. There's plenty of grass in Jones's Strip, outside of my lease."

Herrod's cigar made a fiery parabola through the night as he flung it savagely against the hood of the near wagon, its shower of sparks revealing the cattleman's congested features for a pinched-off instant.

"Back on the Rio Grande, I remember you used to pack a gun, Troy. I'm giving you fair warning to resume the practice if you expect to back up this talk."

Herrod paused, waiting for Troy's reaction. The lean

9

mulewhacker came to his feet, saying to Whitey Crade in a brusque aside, "I'm going to ring that bell again. Damned ferry must have foundered on the way over."

Herrod's rumbling laugh followed Troy over to the landing, but its import failed to penetrate just then. Fred Bolte had picked up his lantern and was teetering his way down the piling stringers as Troy gave the bell rope a yank. Doc Godette stood by, Bolte's fish slung over a warped shoulder.

Herrod called through the dusk, "Tell him, Fred!" and crunched off through the gravel to rejoin the girl who waited alongside the Yakima stage.

"Tell me what, Bolte?" Troy asked sharply, as the bell's reverberations thinned in their ears.

"The boss means you can ring that bell till hell freezes over, I reckon," Bolte grunted, fingering the hooks and flies which decorated his hatband. "The ferry don't cater to freight wagons any more."

The hazy apprehension which had been shaping up in Troy ever since Bix Herrod had mentioned summer graze came into sharp focus in the Texan's brain now. "Who says it don't?"

Doc Godette's chuckle was a thin scraping noise beside him. "Herrod leased the Brewster ferry this afternoon my friend. It will handle stages and hossbackers. But no wagons."

Troy's hand fisted on the bell rope.

"I see. Bolte lit his lantern to signal the ferrytender not to answer my bell, is that it?"

"Not bad guesswork, Troy," Doc Godette commented.

Whitey Crade joined Troy after Bolte and the oldster had returned to the stage depot. "Trouble, Del?"

Troy's answering nod was delayed. He stared angrily

10

across the blue-black ripples of the river, to where the tied-up ferry was a blot against the dancing reflection of Brewster's lights.

"Plenty. Herrod's closed the ferry to us. It's his opening move in a game to freeze us out of Flaming Canyon, partner."

Crade's shoulders lifted and fell. He spat into the darkness, accepting this crushing news without rancor.

"Then we're licked. We can't get Slankard's freight across no other way."

Troy brushed past his partner, heading for the wagons. "If Herrod aims to force a range war, we got to make a stand here and now, he called back. "We'll cross the river tonight."

CHAPTER TWO

FOOLS FOR LUCK

FROM THE JOCKEY-BOX OF HIS LEAD WAGON DEL TROY fished out a coiled shellbelt and a holstered six-gun. Whitey Crade watched apprehensively as his partner buckled on the gun harness, jacked open the Colt, and shoved a .45 cartridge into the empty chamber under the firing-pin.

"Don't let Bix shove you into the wrong stall, now," Crade warned nervously. "He don't strike me as an *hombre* who's let his draw go rusty since he became a range boss. Killin' Herrod won't solve this thing."

Troy crossed around behind the caboose and hauled a double-rigged Brazos saddle from the tailgate. He cinched the rig on his close-coupled steeldust mustang, and slipped the hackamore which trailed his mount.

11

"Getting this jag of freight to Slankard comes first," Troy grunted, swinging into stirrups. "That ferry is a public carrier. Herrod can't discriminate against my trade. I'm going after that ferry."

Crade stared, running splayed fingers through his close-cropped, flax-white hair. "You're loco. If Bolte said the ferry belongs to Herrod, you can bet they ain't bluffing about picking who they'll carry."

Troy curvetted the steelduster away from the caboose. His spine was ramrod straight now, his weariness shed like an unwanted garment before the urgency of his purpose. He stared down at his partner in the thickening gloom of the summer night. "Unhitch and water the mules. If Herrod pulls out for Yakima before I get back, treat yourself to one drink. Otherwise, guard the freight."

Troy touched the mustang with steel and moved off in the night, heading up the river. His departure was masked from the stagecoach depot by intervening cottonwoods and willow brake. Before he drew out of earshot he caught the jangle of whippletrees as Whitey Crade unhooked the tugs.

A half mile upstream, Troy reined down to the water's edge and, loosening his gun belt, hoisted it armpit high and tightened the buckle, in anticipation of the swimming depths ahead.

Directly opposite, to the north, was the sandy promontory which marked the site of the old Astor fur tradingpost. Beyond it the Okanogan River poured its silty flood into the broader blue bend of the Columbia. Both rivers were narrow at the point of confluence, offering no ford, but suitable for the crossing Troy had in mind.

The steelduster dipped its muzzle into the cold water,

protesting as Troy spurred it out into the sluggish back eddies. A moment later the mustang lost footing in the near channel and the gelid river rose over Troy's boots and chap-clad thighs and touched his midriff with a welcome coolness.

The main current caught them then, and the flats where old Fort Okanogan had stood became an impossible objective for the swimming horse. Troy lifted his elbows above the ripples, enjoying the feel of the river against his parched flesh, and wondered if he would have to quit the saddle and cling to the steelduster's tail when they hit the turbulent influx of the Okanogan.

They faced a six mile current in midstream, and it had already swept them abreast of the Port Columbia landing where Crade would be watering the teams. The thick hawsers of the ferry cable made their twin strike overhead, black threads awheel under the star-powdered sky; and then the Texas mustang was quartering toward the west bank, flung downstream like drifting froth by the inexorable current.

Disaster threatened in the rough waters marking the union of the Okanogan and the Columbia as the swimming horse was overwhelmed by the backwash of a sidewheel steamer, churning upstream toward Tonasket. The steelduster was floundering in a desperate, losing fight for survival before an eddy swung them back into slack water abreast of the tied-up ferry.

A sprawl of outjutting gravel south of the Brewster settlement loomed ahead and the steelduster's hoofs finally made purchase on solid bottom. An eternity later horse and rider were ashore, breasting stomach-deep salt cedar scrub and tule growth.

Troy climbed out of saddle, letting the mustang take a breather after its hard battle with the river's cross currents. Mentally he was comparing this mighty seaward-rushing Columbia with the Rio Grande and the Pecos and the Nueces and the other rivers he had fought in the past. Washington's waters, just as Washington's arid desert stretches, outclassed anything Texas had to pit against a man.

He emptied his cowboots, stripped and wrung out his waist Levis and sopping shirt, grateful for the impromptu bath which had revivified his dehydrated tissues. Exhaustion had bogged his spirits on their way out of the scabrock country today; but the anger which charged his veins and the invigorating swim had put the man back in fighting fettle, like some intoxicating drug.

Back in saddle, the .45 snugged down against his hip, Del Troy spurred up to the historic Cariboo Trail which led to the Canadian wilderness and hit the outskirts of Brewster at a high lope.

Avoiding the main street, he followed the water-front shacks to the ferry landing. Against the filigreed pattern of the stars on the mirror-smooth river, he made out the black rectangle of the ferry, tied up at its mooring for the night. The fat twin cables stretched off and away in dwindling perspective toward the far lights marking the Port Columbia stage depot.

Despite Crade's apprehensions, Del Troy was not underestimating the caliber of the enemy he faced. He had known Bix Herrod of old; knew that the fortune which Herrod had brought to Washington Territory a decade ago was the profits of wet cattle shoved across the Rio Grande by the dark of the moon.

He knew of the gun rep which Herrod had left behind on the Texas Trail; knew of the graves which the Lazy

14

H boss had filled in the Panhandle and through the brasada country. He wondered what manner of woman Shasta Ives might be, wishing he had seen Herrod's intended wife in the revealing light of day.

Herrod had planned this showdown tonight. His knowledge of Troy's coup in Flaming Canyon had been telegraphed by his act of closing the Brewster Ferry.

It was a shrewd stroke to cripple Troy at the outset. Without the proceeds of his freighting contracts with Steen Slankard, the Conconully trader, Troy would be unable to develop his homestead. And Herrod, by cutting this essential link across the Columbia which Troy was forced to patronize on his way to and from the outfitting posts at Spokane and Sprague, had struck Troy at the most vulnerable chink in his armor.

These thoughts rode in black procession through Troy's head as he gigged the dripping steelduster down to the shack where Ed Guerrant, the ferryman, had his office and living-quarters. His call brought the old man out of his shack with a lantern.

"Just a hoss an' rider?" Guerrant greeted him disappointedly. "Minimum toll is five bucks, young feller. Wait till mornin' and cross with the Wilbur mail wagon for only six bits. I—"

Guerrant broke off, recognizing the horseman before him in the glare of the uplifted lantern. "Troy! I—uh—"

The oily click of a gunhammer coming to half-cock focused Guerrant's rheumy gaze on the Colt barrel which rested on the Texan's swellfork pommel.

"I know. Herrod's ordered you not to handle my business from here on out." Troy's words held a sinister timbre which belied the laugh that accompanied them. "Get that scow moving, Ed. I got twenty tons of freight waiting on the east bank. Freight that's due in Ruby and

15

Conconully by daylight. You've cost me an hour's delay already."

Guerrant's hand trembled, nearly causing him to drop the lantern. A second premonitory click of the Colt started him down the ramp onto the waiting ferry.

"You can't get away with this high-handed stuff of forcin' a man at gun's point, Troy. There'll be hell to pay when I tell the marshal about this."

Troy rode his mount down to the ferry. It was more raft than boat, being formed of three parallel fir logs with a railed decking of cedar puncheons.

Guerrant cast off his lines and a moment later the ferry groped out of its slip, the current slewing it quarterwise against the tug of the stream, big pulleys humming on overhead cables as the rushing water under the keel logs furnished the motive power to angle the craft across the Columbia.

"Douse your lantern," Troy gruffed from the winchhouse door. "Herrod's over yonder. I wouldn't want you to stop any lead if he took a notion to keep you from landing."

Guerrant hastily complied with the order, extinguishing his lantern as the ferry reached mid-river. He had not lit his running lights and the river was empty of traffic.

The lights of Port Columbia drew closer, vivid against the ebon backdrop of the high plateau behind it. Troy hitched his steelduster to the ferry rail and went forward, eyes drilling the night ahead, gun palmed. His nerves had gone tight again as suspense claimed him, wondering if the guns of Bix Herrod and Doc Godette and Fred Bolte might be waiting out there ahead.

But Whitey Crade was alone on the ferry ramp when the craft nosed between the jutting V of pilings and

16

Guerrant made his bowlines fast. Against the lighted windows of the stage stand, the Conestogas made lurching black shapes as Crade drove the first team aboard. The ferry heeled over under the weight of the overburdened freighters as the mules halted alongside the downstream rail.

"Now the second string, Whitey," Troy ordered softly from the bank where he had stationed himself "Ed, be ready to shove off the instant our last wagon is aboard."

Whitey Crade's big wagons rumbled down onto the ferryboat's deck planks a minute later. Troy heard Shasta Ives's warning shout from the porch of the relay station where the Yakima stage was still waiting.

Ed Guerrant made cursing noises as he lashed his ferry mule into motion, circling the big capstan which, geared to a cable winch, would propel the ferry on its return crossing.

Shouts and the abrasive drumming of feet came out of the night as Troy waited on the landing-ramp, open water widening between him and the ferry's square stern. He saw Fred Bolte loom beside him and attempt to leap aboard the craft, only to meet the down lash of Troy's gun barrel, which dropped the Lazy H gunhawk into knee-deep water inside the slip.

Troy was racing along the piling tops as he heard Bix Herrod and Doc Godette helping Bolte ashore. The Texan leaped for the moving ferry and grabbed the railing for support, bracing his shoulders against the endgate of Crade's trailer.

Then, from the receding blackness of the riverbank, the clotted shadows were breached by the spurt of a muzzle flash and a gunshot flatted through the night, a bullet whining overhead and ripping a slot through a Conestoga hood.

The urge to kill was ground into Troy's mouth as he triggered an answering shot toward the east bank, heard the clamor of shouts which followed.

"Troy's hijacked the boat, by God!" Herrod's shout spanned the widening gap of water. "Doc! Fred! We'll cut the cables and set them adrift!"

Ed Guerrant wailed an oath from the capstan as the overhead cables vibrated to the hewing blows of an ax. One cable sagged and splashed into the river astern, writhing like a boa constrictor against the phosphorescent wake.

"We're done for," the ferryman rasped out as the second cable collapsed, coiling loosely over the upstream rail. "This tub won't stop driftin' short o' the Pacific Ocean."

Troy knew a moment of stark despair as the clumsy barge yawed violently in the turbulent waters, the stern swinging downstream, the lights of Brewster veering crazily around.

Herrod had won. The ferry was at the mercy of the rushing river now, and Troy knew they stood to lose their teams and wagons, perhaps their lives, in the first rapids they would strike.

But a sharp night wind made itself felt on the taut, ribby hoods of the wagons, and the pull and play of cross currents and the sucking vortex of a giant eddy veered them toward the willow-hung banks below Brewster, spinning the forty-foot craft in dizzy carousel until the square prow grated with a grinding shock on the same outjut of gravel where Troy and his horse had landed.

Timbers splintered against submerged rocks and the harness mules brayed their panic into the night as the river drove the ferry hard aground, its deck teetered at a slope which threatened to capsize the overloaded wagons.

Then a final thrust of the whirlpool's rim restored the ferry to an even keel, lodged it with rockbound solidity to the promontory, its beams paralleling the riverbank.

Whitey Crade's voice reached Troy above the clamor of the mules. "We're fools for luck tonight, pardner. We can drive the wagons off onto solid ground up front here."

Guerrant got his lantern lighted and found Del Troy pushing a twenty dollar gold piece into his hands, double the customary toll for the crossing. In accepting the fare, Guerrant forfeited the most valid complaint he could make to the Brewster marshal; but the ferryman turned on Whitey Crade and gloated, "You think you licked Bix Herrod tonight? Hell, your troubles are just beginnin'."

Guerrant saw the albino's enthusiasm fade, and knew a moment's contempt for Crade's puerile ways, his utter ignorance of reality; and he wondered again, as he had wondered in the past, what had brought these oddly contrasted partners together.

"Ed's right about this being the beginning," Troy agreed. "But at least we won the first round."

CHAPTER THREE

LADY GAMBLER

THE WAGONS REACHED THE FORK OF THE MOUNTAIN road just as the gray light of false dawn was touching the morning mists. Because their freight was consigned to different camps, Crade took the Ruby road to the left while Troy pushed on toward Conconully, the county seat.

Dawn was flaming behind the conifer-stippled hill crests when Troy tooled his wagons into the valley pocket between Mineral Hill and the Tarheel and saw the hard angles of the boom camp shaping up through the fog lifting from Salmon Creek.

This was trail's end, and he should have felt exalted by the knowledge that he had delivered this freight in time to meet Slankard's deadline. He had a bonus coming and he had stalled off competing freighters eager to handle Slankard & Company's trade. But the Texan felt only sense of anticlimax, the drag of his own spent forces, the menace which overhung his personal fortunes.

Troy felt a kinship for this brawling backwoods mining town, though he was a cowpuncher and a Texan and, therefore, had two alien counts against him. Most of its buildings had been constructed from lumber which Troy and Crade had hauled over the Cascades from Slankard & Company sawmills on Puget Sound.

The trader had amassed a fortune catering to the building needs of this young and lusty camp. His lumber had gone into the Silver King reduction mill, the Cariboo House hotel, the courthouse; Slankard shingles roofed the saloons and honkies and assay offices. A percentage of those profits had reverted to Troy, giving him the means of developing his homestead at Flaming Canyon, ten miles north.

The sister camp, Ruby, was a primitive settlement with log cabins, dugouts, soddies, and canvas tents. Conconully had an oddly civilized aspect by contrast; its false fronts, its brick bank, gave the county seat an air of solidity, permanence.

As Troy tooled his creaking tandem string down the deserted river of dust which formed the main street, he was struck by a change in Conconully today—an altered expression on the face of the town which he was unable to define.

He saw Sheriff Gaddy winding up his night tour of duty by taking a breakfast tray to the inmates of the county jail. Ambie Pride lay drunk in the alley between Beagle's Saloon and the post office. Otherwise the town seemed deserted, which was an unusual thing even at this hour.

What's happened to this burg? Troy wondered, unhitching his spent mules inside Slankard's stockaded compound. And then he knew. The syndicate's reduction mill was silent. The roar of its stamps, the rumble of its ore hoppers at the far end of town were usually a trembling thunder in the background, day and night, like a waterfall's boom. Today it was strangely mute, leaving a vacuum over the town.

Troy stabled his mules in Slankard's stone barn, groomed and grained his steelduster, and then headed for the trader's office.

He found Slankard at breakfast, a dour, spade-bearded man in late middle life who was well on his way toward being a millionaire.

21

Slankard invited his mulewhacker to join him at the table and he accepted Troy's waybills without enthusiasm. "You made your deadline and I'll pay off with a bonus as agreed," the trader grunted. "But that minin' machinery will rust in my warehouse before I find a buyer."

Pouring himself a cup of coffee, Troy stared at the trader, sensing that some catastrophe must have hit the diggings during his fortnight's absence. "Two weeks ago the mines were begging for this machinery. Crade and I almost killed ourselves getting it here."

Slankard emptied a can of milk over his oatmeal mush. "That was two weeks ago," he said funereally. "Ten days ago a ship landed in Seattle with a ton of gold dust from Alaska. Two-thirds of the miners hereabouts have abandoned their claims and pulled out for the Sound, aiming to book passage for Skagway. This Klondike strike will make the Californy rush of '49 look like chicken feed."

Troy went on eating in silence. Slankard, his appetite gone, went into his front office and returned with a sheaf of greenbacks due his freighters for the Spokane haul. The grim set of Slankard's square-bearded jaw told Troy that this call of gold from the distant Arctic would somehow touch his own destiny.

"Where does all this leave the Okanogan boom, Steen?"

Slankard counted out the currency before answering. "It means Conconully and Ruby will be ghost towns by fall, son. Maybe you and Crade were right, plantin' your flag on a cattle spread instead of staking out a mining claim like I advised when you first hit this country."

Troy pondered the trader's grim prediction, knowing that Steen Slankard was not given to rash judgments

22

where they concerned his own business future. Slankard was a big operator, owner of half the enterprises in Ruby and the county seat, a man who controlled vast holdings of Puget Sound timberland and whose power in the State was rivaled only by the squaw man up on the Twenty-Mile Strip, Okanogan Jones.

"I'm sending you over to Coulee City tomorrow to pick up a load of trade goods from a store I bought out," Slankard said. "That will probably be the last business I'll be able to send your way, Troy. Slankard & Company will probably pull out of the diggings before the summer is over."

Troy built a cigarette, his mind reeling under the implications of this news. If Slankard went out of business, it meant that Troy's sole source of revenue was cut off, with his savings far short of the minimum he and Whitey Crade had deemed sufficient to stock their prospective ranch in Flaming Canyon.

He thought of Bix Herrod, and his impending showdown with the powerful Lazy H outfit—and the realization of what this body blow meant to his own prospects put a brassy taste on his tongue.

"If this Coulee City haul will add to your losses, Steen, forget it. Consider my contract with you cancelled."

Slankard tilted back his chair and thrust thumbs to armpits. A brooding speculation touched the trader's face as he regarded the hard-bitten young Texan.

"Bix Herrod has been scouting your range over in Flaming Canyon this week, Del," Slankard drawled. "Might be you could sell out to the Lazy H and recover what you've sunk in that homestead during the past two years."

Troy touched a match to his cigarette and pulled in a

deep drag of smoke. He put on his Stetson and stood up to leave. "I ran across Herrod at Brewster Ferry last night," he said laconically. "Herrod already knows Flaming Canyon graze won't be open for his beef."

Leaving Slankard's, Troy crossed the Salmon Creek bridge and made his way to the Cariboo House, where he maintained a room for such times as he was not living on his homestead.

Sleep blotted out his senses the moment he sprawled out on his bunk; and when he awakened, the weltering sunrays of late afternoon were shafting through the window, and he realized he had slept out the entire day.

He dressed and shaved and left the hotel, making his way to the Loop-Loop Casino on the main street. Shouldering through the batwings, he found the big gambling hall almost deserted.

Ordinarily the Loop-Loop's roulette layout and poker tables would be doing a heavy business this time of evening. Now, he found only one game going—Roxanna Laranjo's blackjack concession.

He watched the raven-haired girl, her vivid scarlet gown standing out against the smoky shadows of the deadfall, her dusky hands shuffling and dealing cards with a supple grace. The chance of talking privately with Roxanna Laranjo brought Troy his first relief and anticipation since his return to the diggings.

The girl's lustrous black eyes lighted in recognition as the Texan moved toward her table, and she turned to the quartet of miners and said, "This game is closed, gentlemen."

She cashed her customer's chips and came over to a corner table where Troy had seated himself.

"It's good to see you back, Del. A lot has happened since you left for Spokane."

24

Troy helped her into a barrel chair and toyed with the gold bangles which adorned her slim, olive-skinned wrists. "Seems I always cry on your shoulder when trouble breaks for me," he grinned. "Slankard's canceled the summer business I been counting on. This Alaska gold rush has put a bad crimp in my outlook, Roxie."

He drank strength from the sympathy in the girl's eyes. In a land where women plied an older and more dubious profession, Roxanna Laranjo stood out as a nugget amid dross. "That lady gambler at the Loop-Loop," the local miners had dubbed her. She had handled the blackjack concession at the Casino for a year now, fraternizing with the rough element who patronized the place, yet keeping herself rigidly aloof.

A girl of mixed Spanish and Chihuahuan blood, Troy had first known this amazing woman back on the Rio Grande. Between them, from the first, had been a rapport which transcended the usual physical bond between a man and a woman on the frontier. Always she had been remote and unattainable, oblivious to the healthy hungers which her beauty aroused in Del Troy.

She had been a dancer in a Laredo fandango house in the old days. Their paths had separated, and somewhere during the ten years which had followed, Roxanna had brushed the sharp edges of life and a disillusionment bordering on bitterness had caused her to become a professional gambler, mysterious and introspective.

Yet always, as now, Troy found his spirit buoyed by the very nearness of this exotic, dusky-skinned beauty. He found in her personality a platonic affinity he had never known for any other woman in his life.

"Bix Herrod aims to summer his beef in Flaming Canyon, Del," the girl said suddenly, withdrawing her hand from his.

25

He met the full strike of Roxanna's black eyes and thought he read a mixture of fear and anxiety blended in their depths.

"I know," he mused, and told her of last night's episode at Brewster Ferry.

"If he'll buy you and Crade out, you must sell," Roxie burst out passionately when he had finished. "Herrod will stop at nothing to gain control of your Canyon, Del. The girl he plans to marry wants to graze her cattle on the range you've leased from Okanogan Jones. That much is common knowledge around Conconully."

He moved his chair around the table to be closer to her and she saw the cedar-butted gun belted at his flank, something which had escaped her attention as he crossed the room a few moments ago.

"You know what Flaming Canyon means to me, Roxie," he told her gently. "It's not like you to ask me to quit when the going gets rough. Why should I give up the choicest cattle range in Washington State? It's mine. I'll fight to hold it."

Beads of sweat had broken out on Roxanna Laranjo's olive forehead, and her firmly rounded bosom rose and fell to the violence of her breathing.

"You haven't packed a gun since you came West," she murmured. "I take that to mean that sooner or later you will face Bix Herrod in a shoot-out. I don't want that to happen, *querido mio.*"

The Mexican endearment fell strange on Del Troy's ears, after so long away from Texas, and brought vivid memories flooding through him, making him wonder again what vagary of destiny had brought this girl to a back-of-beyond mining camp like Conconully.

Whatever dark and brooding secret her past held,

Troy did not know, nor did he seek to invade her privacy on the strength of their long-standing friendship. It would have pleased him to think that she followed him out West, but he knew that was not the case. Roxanna had never shared so much as a kiss with him, though she must have known that love for her could be an easy thing to arouse in him.

"If Herrod aims to make a range war of this thing," Troy bit out, "then he shall have it. Not one Lazy H or Dollar cow will graze on Flaming Canyon grass as long as I'm alive to prevent it, Roxie. I have told Herrod as much."

The girl's hand shook visibly as she plucked at a slender gold chain which encircled her neck, and from the cleft of her bosom she drew a small crucifix and a plain gold band which Troy had never seen before. It was a wedding ring, and it struck him in that instant as a clue to whatever loss had extinguished the vivacity Roxanna Laranjo had once shown the world.

"You must not fight such odds as Herrod will put against you, *amigo*," she whispered. "For you it would only mean a bullet from ambush. That is the way Bix Herrod fights."

Troy did not appear to have heard her foreboding words. "I visited the Indian agent over at Nespelem last week," he said. "The agency is ready to buy all the beef I can raise. The Colville Reservation is the largest in this part of the United States. Which means that making Flaming Canyon pay off is not a gamble. I'd be a fool to give it up."

Roxanna shook her lovely head, wise to the ways of this man before her, bowing to the adamant purpose which controlled his life, knowing the measure of his courage and his inflexible decision.

27

"You'll fight this Herrod," she predicted, "and you'll lose. Men as fine and true and stanch as you have fought him and lost, *compañero.*"

She signaled the bartender for a glass of chianti then, and changed the subject to more trivial things. It was a right-angle departure from her previous trend of talk, but he left her an hour later with the feeling that Roxanna had known Bix Herrod in the past more intimately than Troy himself had known the Texas cattleman.

CHAPTER FOUR

"EVERY MAN HAS HIS PRICE"

TROY WAS IN THE SADDLE BEFORE DAYLIGHT HAD thinned the gray mists next morning, feeling the need of paying his haying crews a visit in Flaming Canyon before starting on Slankard's week-long junket to Coulee City.

He covered the ten miles of mining road to the rimrock overlooking his homestead in time to catch the full strike of dazzling sunrise on the obsidian cliffs of the canyon, and as always the spectacle stirred him to the core of his being.

The genesis of Flaming Canyon's name was rooted deep in Indian legendry—the description given it by some prehistoric huntsman who had marveled at the fire-bright glare of dawn refracting from its fluted scarps.

The cliffs gave off that illusion of pulsing incandescence this morning, exactly as they had done on a morning three years ago when Del Troy and his albino partner, Whitey Crade, had passed this way on their way toward a Canadian cariboo hunt.

A cowman born and bred, Troy had recognized this vast rock-hemmed range as a veritable stockman's Eden. Its velvet-green expanse was watered by Glacier Creek, a meandering stream which sluiced down the long gorge like a ribbon of platinum, feeding on the everlasting ice of the high Cascades, a permanent guarantee against the blight of summer droughts.

Troy, like Crade, had been a drover for a big Texas combine a year before their arrival here. They had hazed longhorns to Montana and Wyoming and, yielding to mutually itching feet, had crossed the Bitterroots out of Idaho to explore the unsettled reaches of Washington State.

From the moment of his first glimpse of Flaming Canyon, Del Troy was aware that he faced a crossroads in his life. His twenties had been spent with irresponsible drifting, responding to urges to see what lay over the next hill. A hundred widely separated cow camps had known him. It had been an unfettered life, free and wild, sometimes dangerous, but never boring.

But with his thirtieth birthday behind him, Troy sensed that he had come to the point in a man's life where driving his picket pin on a spread of his own was something that could not be long delayed if he ever achieved anything beyond a tumbleweed's roaming existence.

Whitey Crade, five years younger and still at the peak of his wanderlust, had responded dubiously to Troy's enthusiasm over Flaming Canyon; but he had agreed to postpone their cariboo hunt and followed Troy back to the Conconully land office to investigate the possibilities of filing on a homestead.

Before that summer was done they had erected cabins on contiguous 160-acre claims under the provisions of the Donation Land Act. Money to develop their embryo ranch was their first need, and a freighting contract with Steen Slankard had supplied that.

Directly behind their homestead boundaries, Flaming Canyon's sheer cliffs narrowed like an hourglass, the connecting notch known as Keyhole Pass. Beyond the Keyhole, the Canyon widened to as much as five miles from rim to rim, snaking northwesterly into the country known as the Twenty-Mile Strip which Congress had set aside from the Indian lands they had opened to white settlement.

Except for an unfired section of public domain at Keyhole Pass, ownership of Flaming Canyon's upper range was vested in the hands of the celebrated Osoyoos Lake pioneer, Cyrus "Okanogan" Jones. Troy had had little difficulty in getting a year's lease on Flaming Canyon's entire length from Jones, with an option to renew it annually as his ranch expanded; for the squaw man at Osoyoos Lake was interested primarily in future speculation of timber and mineral rights on the Strip.

Given time and the Indian agency's market for his beef, Troy was confident he could transform Flaming Canyon into a spread which would rival the big outfits at Yakima and Ellensburg. This coming fall would see the importation of bulls and she-stock to form the nucleus of his future herd.

Reining up on the rimrock overlooking the twin homesteads, Troy hipped over in saddle and let his eye follow the eroded walls of volcanic glass which twisted their serpentine way into the haze-filled timberland of the Twenty-Mile Strip, with the Canadian Rockies sprawled in remote, brooding grandeur on the northern horizon.

From this elevation he could see the tents of his hay crew pitched on the edge of Glacier Creek where it entered the notch of Keyhole Pass. In the hayland beyond he could see a dozen wagons topheavy with cut hay, crawling turtlelike down the road toward their homesteads.

The ricks were driven by jean-clad, straw-hatted nesters from the belt of farmland which covered the Okanogan River valley from Malotte to Tanesket. These farmers were at work harvesting the hay crop which would winter their own horses and milk cows, as well as the beef cattle Troy intended to bring up this fall.

Directly below him, Troy scanned his log ranch house and the neat, whitewashed corrals and outbuildings which he and Crade had built during the past year. A mile across the sprawling mouth of the canyon, close to the north cliffs, a smaller shack marked Whitey Crade's homestead. A wisp of smoke was spiraling from the rock chimney there, proof that Crade had returned home after unloading Slankard's freight at Ruby yesterday.

Troy put his horse down the steep road into the canyon, circled his homestead grounds, and crossed the flats to Keyhole Pass. A half mile beyond the nesters' tents he approached a bucolic hayshaker riding a mowing machine.

A notch of worry furrowed the farmer's sun-blackened visage as the Texas cowman pulled up beside his team.

"How's it going, Dreyfuss?"

The farmer climbed from his bucket seat to extricate a mangled rattlesnake from his cutter bar. His rheumy eyes avoided Troy as he answered in a Hoosier's drawl, "Figger the canyon will yield a ton an' a half, mebbe

31

two tons of prime hay to the acre, Mr. Troy. If we can harvest it, that is."

Troy cuffed back his Stetson, sensing that trouble had visited the hay crews in advance of his own arrival here.

"Why not? I own this grass. We'll split fifty-fifty on every ton you cut. Don't the deal satisfy you and your neighbors?"

Dreyfuss waved at a passing hayrick, bound for a farm on the river bottom east of Flaming Canyon.

"We're not tryin' to hedge out on our bargain, son. Us hoe men are grateful for this hay. But a passel of gunslingers rode in from Yakima day before yesterday. Ordered us to leave this grass stand for cattle they aim to summer here."

Troy laughed harshly. Bix Herrod had left his hint of gunsmoke reprisal behind him, then, in an effort to intimidate these rustic sodbusters into abandoning the hay harvest.

"I know. But you'll get your hay if I have to bring in troops from Fort Colville to fight off those Yakima range hogs, Dreyfuss. Keep your rakes and mowers on the job. I'll handle the policing of this canyon."

Dreyfuss climbed back on his mower, mopped his grimy face with a faded bandanna, and scowled moodily. "I got a wife and kids to think about, Mr. Troy. Don't count on me or ary o' my neighbors toting a rifle along with our pitchforks. Most of us lost our homes because of cattle wars back in Nebrasky and Kansas. I for one don't aim to get mixed up in no shootin' fracas."

Troy put his horse around and headed out of the Keyhole, overhauled the outbound haywagon at a gallop, and reined up finally at the gate of Whitey Crade's yard.

His partner emerged from the cabin as Troy was

32

watering the steelduster down by the creek. Daylight revealed the strange physical appearance which had warped Whitey Crade's personality.

An albino, Crade's hair was the dead white of carded cotton fibers; his lashes and brows were so thin and colorless as to give his milky face a naked, grotesque appearance. No amount of rain or sun or wind could darken the fish-belly pallor of his skin. His eyes were the deep pink of a rabbit's, and it was this freakish lack of pigmentation which had tainted Whitey Crade's entire life, warped his philosophy, made him belligerent and neurotic in all his human relationships.

It was a strange, almost macabre partnership, this bond between Whitey Crade and Del Troy. It had had its beginnings on a trail drive to Dodge, five years before. A foray by a Comanche war party had stampeded the herd after their crossing of the Red, and Crade had been trapped in the path of the longhorn juggernaut.

Troy, acting as trail boss, had swung an unerring rope to pluck his albino flank rider from certain death. And Crade's pathetic, almost childish gratitude had been the basis of their partnership. From that moment on, Crade had attached himself like a leech to the whippy-built trail boss; and Troy, seeing an opportunity to salvage something from a drifting human derelict who was a victim of his own complexes, had brought Crade west with him.

In their Flaming Canyon homesteads, Troy had seen a means of giving the albino some worth-while purpose for living, some shield for his tottering sanity.

The partnership had been a cross for Troy to bear from the first. Crade's basic moral structure was unstable. He was given to strong drink and gambling; he had a predilection for bad women and gunplay which had brought their partnership to the verge of a break on more than one occasion. Only a deep, underlying sense of pity and responsibility toward a weakling had given Troy the forbearance necessary to keep their friendship on a going basis.

"Drinking again, Whitey?" Troy greeted bluntly, noting the bleary glaze on Crade's ruby irises, the unsteadiness of his gait as the albino lurched down the slope from the front gate. "I thought I told you to lay off booze. A man who can't handle his likker and tries to pick a fight every time he—"

Crade grabbed a hitching-post for support, his breath coming in gusty whistles. "Damn it, you're packin' a gun. Why don't you use it? Afraid it'll git tangled in yore apron strings?"

Troy sucked in a slow, deep breath, curbing the anger that seethed close to the surface as he saw Whitey Crade's splayed fingers poise above the stock of a side-hammer Root .36 at his hip. Knowing Crade's mercuric temperament, Troy had long since exacted a promise from the cowboy never to tote a gun, drunk or sober.

"Pull in your horns, Whitey. I dropped by to tell you that our summer contract with Slankard & Company is washed up."

It was stunning news, spelling catastrophe for everything they had slaved to build up here in Flaming Canyon—but Crade's chalky face wrinkled in a grin, his recent passion ebbing from him as quickly as it had flared up.

"*'Sta bueno* by me. Never liked mulewhackin' nohow."

Troy's eye ranged along the barbed-wire drift fence which blocked off the mouth of Flaming Canyon, marking the common boundary of their homesteads.

34

That fence was the tangible barrier which would face the pool herd which Shasta Ives and Bix Herrod were pushing up the trail from Yakima.

Disregarding his partner's callous indifference to their dilemma, Troy stepped into saddle.

"I'm pulling out this afternoon with one wagon," he said, "heading for Coulee City on the last run we'll make for Slankard. I want you to water my tomato vines and milk the cow while I'm gone. And I want you to stick close to the spread until I get back, do you understand?"

A humility touched Whitey Crade, his usual reaction of remorse chastening him after a flare-up at his partner's discipline. "You can depend on me to do the chores, Del. I ain't forgettin' you saved my life back in Oklahoma. You're an *hombre* to ride the river with, Del."

Annoyance carved a crease between Troy's eyes as he picked up his reins for the return ride to Conconully.

"I wish you'd forget that Oklahoma business, Whitey. You don't owe me a thing. We're pardners. That's enough."

Whitey Crade's mouth slackened into a doltish grin as he watched Del Troy ride off across the canyon floor, pass his homestead grounds, and vanish beyond the far cliffs.

Then, touched by the backlash of his own unpredictable emotions, Crade squared his shoulders and headed back to his cabin. Waiting at a deal table there were Bix Herrod and the ubiquitous Doc Godette, the oldster clad in a Confederate battle tunic whose brass buttons carried the tarnish of thirty-odd years since Appomattox.

"Troy's heading for Coulee City, eh?" the Lazy H

35

boss remarked, picking up a whisky bottle from the table as Whitey Crade pushed the door wide open behind him and stood glowering at his two visitors. "Have another drink, Whitey."

Crade brushed a hand across his flabby mouth, dropped it to squeeze the butt of his .36. "Get out of here!" he snarled waspishly. "I've changed my mind. Ought to be hoss-whipped for even givin' a second thought to your offer to buy out this homestead. If I'd swilled much more o' that rotgut, you'd a' talked me into double-crossin' the best pardner a man ever had."

Bix Herrod appraised the albino, pursed his lips thoughtfully, and then got to his feet.

"Let's drift, Doc. Señor Crade ain't in a mood to talk business this morning, I take it."

Crade stood aside as his visitors left the cabin.

"And don' be comin' back with your bottles o' snake pizen," he shrieked, a sob trembling in his voice. "I ain't sellin' out my land, come hell or high water. Troy an' me control Flamin' Canyon an' we don't aim to let go our hold to no Yakima range hog."

Herrod and Doc Godette walked over to Crade's lean-to barn and let out the saddle horses they had rented in Brewster the day before. Concealing the horses where Del Troy had missed seeing them was a precaution which Herrod had occasion to be thankful for.

On their way through the wire gate which the outbound haywagon crew had neglected to close behind them, Doc Godette eyed his companion quizzically, unable to fathom the complacent grin which Bix Herrod had carried away from their abortive interview with Troy's partner.

"Looks to me like we got some wire-cutting ahead of us, Bix," the medico commented. "Buying a hundred-

and-sixty-acre right-o'-way into Flaming Canyon ain't in the cards."

Herrod grinned expansively. "I haven't played my ace in the hole yet, Doc. I'll send Shasta over to dicker with Crade tomorrow. She'll cool him down."

Godette scowled and kept his secret thoughts to himself.

"Every man ever born has his price," Herrod went on. "Crade's price won't come high, especially when Shasta goes to work on him. That albino pimp will open a quarter-section hole into Flaming Canyon before our trail herd sights this fence. You can bet your last blue chip on that, my friend."

Doc Godette lapsed into a coughing spell which left him spent and gasping. A medical man, he knew he carried his own death sentence in his diseased lungs, that time was running short for him.

"I hope so," he wheezed. "Troy's got the law on his side. It'll take more than bluff or gunsmoke to pry our way into Flaming Canyon this summer. Mebbe Shasta's your answer. But I doubt it."

CHAPTER FIVE

AMBUSHED

AT THREE O'CLOCK DEL TROY PULLED OUT OF Slankard's compound with a payload of kegged nails and tarpaper rolls in his single wagon, consigned to the Indian Agency at Nespelem.

A depression lay on his spirit, engendered by Steen Slankard's gloomy forecast of Conconully becoming a ghost town by fall, and Roxie Laranjo's prescience that

37

a finish fight with Bix Herrod would end disastrously for him.

Roxie, provocative in a satin dressing-robe, stood framed by the upper gallery door of the Loop-Loop as he swung the mule string out into the deserted street, and her smile was erased from her lips as she saw the stock of a Winchester booted under his saddle fender.

That rifle usually reposed under the seat of the Conestoga, a weapon carried solely for the purpose of bagging game to supplement Troy's rations on a long haul through primitive country. Its presence alongside his pommel now told the girl that Del Troy had drawn stakes in a game which necessitated his being ready for any emergency he might meet, day or night, from now on.

A block beyond the Loop-Loop, Troy was startled out of his lethargy by hearing a feminine voice hail him by name from the wooden-awninged porch of the Cariboo House. Aside from Roxanna Laranjo, there were no women to be found closer than Straight-Edge Lulu's bawdy house in Ruby. Troy halted his team and peered curiously at the hotel.

A young woman in her early twenties, wearing a flat-crowned marbled Stetson, work shirt, and split riding-skirt, came down the steps and crossed the foot bridge over the creek, her spurred boots spraying little puffs of dust as she halted before him.

He had never seen her around the diggings before, he was certain; her beauty was too striking to have been overlooked in this thoroughly masculine camp, and he mentally ticketed her as the wife of some visiting engineer. A wealth of burnished wheat-gold hair cascaded to her shoulders, in vivid contrast to the deep amber brown of her eyes.

Not until he saw the dollar sign worked out in brass studs on her belt did he realize that he was facing Shasta Ives, whom he remembered only as a vague outline at the Port Columbia stage depot two nights before. Her ranch derived its brand from the superimposed initials of her late father, Sam Ives, which formed the Dollar symbol, $.

"Didn't take the stage south the other night, eh, ma'am?"

His greeting was couched in a dry humor which brought a slight flush to her cheeks. He scanned the girl's supple figure in bold appraisal, mentally approving the lift of her firm young breasts under the faded shirt, the even whiteness of her teeth.

"Mr. Troy, if you can spare a moment I'd like to discuss something with you. Something vitally important to both of us."

Hat on saddlehorn, a cigarette curling smoke between the fingers of his left hand, Troy's eyes hardened into bleak slits. "As Bix Herrod's intended bride, I reckon you want to discuss summer graze, ma'am. That issue is closed tighter'n a pair of mail-order boots, so far as Flaming Canyon is concerned."

Shasta Ives's dark eyes glittered, putting a vitality there which added to her natural attraction. The unblinking intensity of her gaze told Troy that, although this girl was an enemy of all that meant anything to his life, she was a woman of unquestioned charm, and therefore doubly dangerous.

"Aren't you being a—a dog in the manger, Mr. Troy?" she asked accusingly. "You know the drought has burned up Yakima range this year. Lazy H and Dollar have to get summer graze or face a die-off before round-up. As I understand it, you aren't running a single steer in Flaming Canyon."

Troy remained untouched by her logic, the thought needling him that Herrod was behind this meeting, using the girl as a go-between to gain his objectives.

"I'm not a dog in the manger, Miss Ives. I'm not letting Flaming Canyon grass go to seed. It's being harvested to tide me over the winter. Crade and I hope to stock the canyon by fall."

The girl made circles in the dust with a dainty boot toe. "Couldn't we—Mr. Herrod and I—rent the use of your grazing range until our October beef gather?"

"What's the matter with the graze outside the Canyon? Okanogan Jones owns half the Strip from the river to the Cascade divide. He'll lease you whatever your herd needs."

Shasta bit her lip, anger showing in her eyes now.

"You know how rough the Strip country is, Mr. Troy. Inside your Canyon, a dozen riders could keep our cattle bunched all summer. It—it's only fair to warn you, Mr. Troy—Bix has used Flaming Canyon in the past and he will again. Until you actually have stock to feed on that grass, Bix feels that you have no legal right to deny us grazing rights."

Troy donned his sombrero and yanked his jerkline.

"*Adios,* ma'am. I don't think Herrod has any doubts as to where the legal rights lie in this case."

Shasta Ives jumped back to avoid the heavy wheels of the Conestoga, and her defiant shout lashed up at him. "You cut a wide swath now, Mr. Troy. If Bix wanted to he could sue you for your last dollar, for wrecking the ferry he leased from Ed Guerrant down in Brewster."

Troy's retort reached her through the whorling dust: "That ferry wouldn't have been wrecked if Bix and his friends hadn't cut the cables, ma'am."

He crossed the Okanogan by way of the Omak Ford at dusk, and camped that night at the Disautel Claim deep in the Colville Indian reservation.

The next day he unloaded Slankard's freight at the Nespelem agency and turned his mules due south, to cross the Columbia at Wild Goose Bill's ferry the following morning. This third day on the road would find him bucking the sun-baked scab-rock badlands on the high, sage-scented desert plateau.

He derived no comfort from the knowledge that this was probably the last time he would have to endure the ordeal of crossing the Basin desert. The cancellation of a lucrative summer freight contract with Steen Slankard, due to the unforeseen exodus of miners to the Yukon gold rush, had come as a crippling blow to Troy's dreams.

Every passing hour drew Bix Herrod's trail herd closer to an open showdown at the entrance of Flaming Canyon. Facing the Lazy H gun-hung crew loomed as a tough prospect, for Troy was virtually playing a lone-wolf game.

He knew he could not depend on the loyalty of Whitey Crade if the showdown involved a gun fight with Lazy H. Sheriff Irv Gaddy, the law of Conconully, would back him to the limit, he knew; but having the government behind him would be of scant help if Herrod breached the homestead fence and shoved two or three thousand head of hungry cattle onto Flaming Canyon grass.

A second visit from Herrod's emissaries to the hay harvesters would result inevitably in the river bottom farmers pulling out of Flaming Canyon en masse. That would leave his lease wide open to the inroads of the Yakima steers, and by the time he could get a restraining injunction filed against Herrod in the circuit court, the damage would be irreparable.

By mid-day, Troy was faced by the abyss of Grand Coulee, forcing him to veer southwestward across the bitter expanse of sage and greasewood and lava outcrops. His destination, the railhead of Coulee City, lay across a break in the great chasm near the Dry Falls.

Lack of forage for the mules forced Troy to abandon travel during the heat of the afternoon. He doled out water to the suffering brutes from the barrel he had filled at the Columbia River. As soon as dusk came he hitched up and pushed on.

A full moon rode the cloudless sky and its argentine glow threw the four-hundred-foot cliffs of Dry Falls into vivid, awesome relief as Troy's wagon skirted the one-time cascade where the waters of the Columbia, thrown out of their original bed by the action of glaciers and prehistoric earthquakes, had once formed a cataract by which the glories of Niagara would be reduced to a seeping trickle by comparison.

The old bed of the river made rough going for the wagon, but the lights of Coulee City lifted above the far horizon and Del Troy was determined to keep the mules going all night if need be, to achieve his goal short of another scorching day.

He was dozing in saddle when, from the clotted shadows of a scab-rock outcrop at the brink of Dry Falls, the cool night was cracked by the shattering roar of a gunshot.

A bullet whipped past Troy's cheek as he straightened in saddle. He moved by instinct then, snaking the Winchester from his scabbard and leaving the stirrups in a rolling dive.

Muzzle flame from a rifle bore lanced the darkness

ahead of the spooked mules as Troy sprinted for the shelter of his wagon box, and an invisible force sledged his left shoulder and slammed him face forward on the rubble.

Pulling himself to his knees, Troy groped to recover his fallen .30-.30 and levered a shell into the breech. Gunsmoke tarried above the lava outcrop where the dry-gulcher was hidden, its smudging umbrella haloed by the moonbeams.

Troy drove an answering shot in that direction, heard his copper-jacketed bullet ricochet into the awful blackness of the Lower Coulee.

A yell somewhere behind him warned Troy that he was boxed in between cross-firing guns, that he was silhouetted against the white canvas of the Conestoga hood.

Crouched low, Troy headed in the only direction left open to him—toward the brink of the Dry Falls. Bullets quested after his darting body from two angles as he flung himself into a patch of bubble-pitted lava on the very lip of the chasm.

The mules stampeded for fifty yards and came to a halt in a shallow coulee near the outcrop where the first bushwhack shot had breached the night.

Not until he tried to rest his Winchester barrel across a lava chunk did Troy realize that he had been hit. A numbing sensation was spreading down his arm, across his left shoulder, and his fingers came away sticky with a warm, viscid ooze when he explored under his shirt. After this first numbness of bullet shock left him, he knew that a searing agony would set in, reducing his own effectiveness at bagging a target.

At least two bushwhackers were converging on the Conestoga now. Above the tom-tomming in his ears,

43

Troy caught a liquid sloshing sound, and a vagrant breeze brought the fumes of spilled coal oil to his nostrils.

Troy lowered himself to the sanctuary of a yard-wide ledge below the rim, knowing shoot-out was soon to come. His flesh crawled at the prospect of toppling into the empty depths under his right elbow. Half a thousand feet below he saw the twin lakes of stagnant water below the cliff talus, reflecting the high-riding moon like the eyes of a corpse.

Discarding his Stetson, Troy lifted his head above the rimrock in time to see a spurt of ruddy flame blossom in the night as his attackers set fire to the wagon.

If this was an ordinary hold-up by desert bandits out to loot a passing freighter, it seemed unlikely that they would be bent on destroying the empty wagon in this fashion. He saw the mules break into a stampede, panicked by the flames which enveloped the prairie schooner.

Horror bit into Troy as he saw the team veer to the right, headed for the yawning chasm brink.

Seconds later the team went over the edge, the Conestoga teetering against the moonlit sky, its hood blazing like a torch. Nausea crawled into the pit of Troy's stomach as he watched the long, plummeting drop of the ten-mule team and the big wagon, hurtling like a comet down the vertical wall of the Dry Falls toward the broken talus which sloped to meet the prehistoric lakes in the pit of the gorge.

The flaming Conestoga seemed to explode as it struck bottom. An eternity later, it seemed, the appalling crash of mules and wagon volleyed up from the shadow-blocked depths to assault Troy's ears as he crouched, numb and bleeding, on the ledge far above.

44

CHAPTER SIX

THE END OF A FISHERMAN

"PLAY THIS CLOSE TO YORE CHEST, NOW!" CAME A guttural voice through the hushed quiet. "Troy's hit, but he ain't out of the fight by a damned sight. He's trapped on the rim yonder."

The voice struck a familiar chord in Troy's memory, but he couldn't identify its owner. He pushed the carbine aside in favor of his Colt six-gun, knowing his left arm would soon be paralyzed and that the .45 would serve him best in a close-in fight.

He unknotted the bandanna from his neck and snapped the dust out of it, wadding it into a makeshift compress. His hand shook as he unbuttoned his shirt and explored under it, feeling the slow well of blood where a slug had ripped the egg of muscle high on his left arm, near the point of his shoulder. The bone had not been nicked; the wound was more painful than serious.

The abrasive sound of a hobbed boot sole on lava reached his ears but the tricky shift of the breeze made it impossible to orient the direction of the ambusher's movement. The moon put the ground line in sharp relief and Troy waited for the shape of a skulking attacker to cross it.

The bandanna stemmed the flow of blood down his sleeve. He eared the knurled hammer of his Peacemaker to full cock, his eyes raking the rimrock along the full arc of his vision.

A long period of nerve-sapping waiting followed. Occasionally the furtive sounds of his attackers deploying into position for shoot-out reached his ears.

Cicadas trilled in the bunch grass thickets. Somewhere far off a coyote bayed at the moon.

Something twitched the twigs of a greasewood clump directly above the ledge where Troy was cornered. But he held his fire, not sure if a gust of wind had caused the foliage to move.

Farther to his right, metal scraped on rock. A stalking gunman was bellying across the ground, thrusting a rifle ahead of him. Too late, Troy realized that the moonlight had swung around enough to put his ledge under the full betraying glare of its beams. He was a prime target now.

The wind died off. The cloying scent of sage bit into Troy's nostrils. Overhead a shooting star scratched its white, dissolving spark across the heavens. Far below him the shattered wreckage of the Conestoga had started a brush fire, the smell of smoke lifting in an acrid chimney current up the cliff.

The greasewood clump vibrated again, and moonlight glinted off the muzzle of a Springfield rifle thrust tentatively through the foliage.

Troy calculated the angle of the gun, knew that the man behind its sights had not yet spotted his hide-out. He steadied his Colt barrel on the ledge rim and squeezed off a shot.

On the heels of the whipcrack report, Troy heard a brief threshing noise in the gravel behind the greasewood, the gagging exhalations of a man. Spur chains jingled as boot toes made a rataplan on the flinty rubble, and then the noises ceased. The black muzzle of the .45-70 still protruded from the fork of the greasewood bush, canted toward the moon.

Maybe he had dropped a man; maybe it was a ruse to draw him out of hiding to become a target for the second ambusher.

He heard a whisper, "You hit?" But no answer. Then came the furtive sound of a man crawling on all fours directly above him, invisible behind the rimrock. The noise ceased in the vicinity of the greasewood, and a low, dismayed oath reached Troy's ears.

Pain was mounting steadily in Troy's shoulder now, forcing him to grind his teeth against crying out and betraying his position. The shadows altered imperceptibly along the fluted rocks as the moon cruised down the Washington sky. He estimated that a full hour had dragged by before another noise reached him.

It was the drumroll of horse's hoofs, headed southwest. Two horses, traveling across the scoriated channel of the dry riverbed. The ring of steel-shod hoofs on volcanic rock gradually dwindled and left a brooding silence over the empty land.

This sound of a withdrawal posed a problem for Del Troy. The horses might have belonged to passing cavalry scouts bound for some army post, or they might have been the mounts belonging to his ambushers. A wrong guess now would be fatal.

It did not seem likely that his ambushers would withdraw, leaving him in possession of the field. He was too cagey to take for granted that his bullet had tallied a target.

The Springfield left hanging in the greasewood could be bait to lure him out of hiding. On the other hand without so much as a pocket of shadow to take concealment in, Troy knew it would be suicidal to wait until one or the other of the gunmen crawled around the perimeter of dry Falls and cut him down at long range.

Thrusting his throbbing left arm through his shirt front to support it, Troy came to a kneeling position, flesh braced against the expected shock of point-blank lead.

But nothing stirred on the skyline. Crickets sang their sedative lullaby from the sage clumps. The night was so still he could hear the crackle of the fire which was licking the dead grass at the bottom of the coulee.

Taking the long gamble, Troy climbed off the ledge which had been his sanctuary and inched closer to the greasewood, out of line of the .45-70 muzzle. Veering a dozen yards to the left, he topped the hump and had his first look behind the greasewood clump.

A sprawled shape made an angular blot in the shadow of the greasewood. The smell of blood in Troy's nostrils was most likely his own, but he saw the moon refracted in a diamond point from a crawling black puddle beside the formless shadow.

Searching the broken riverbed beyond, Troy finally made up his mind as to the shape events had taken. He had downed one of the bushwhackers with a lucky shot; the remaining gunman had elected to beat a retreat rather than run the risk of a siege.

Standing up, thumb alert on gunhammer, Troy moved forward and halted beside the body which lay in the grotesque posture of death beside the greasewood. A cowboy, judging from the batwing chaps which encased the saddle-warped legs, and the steeple-peaked Stetson which had rolled to one side.

With a boot toe Troy rolled the slack, loose weight of the corpse over on its back. His bullet had smashed the stalker dead center of the forehead, and a curtain of blood and dirt masked the contorted face. The jutting beaver teeth under a blood-clotted ram's horn mustache were vaguely familiar to him.

Then, glancing at the dead man's hat, Troy tagged his

victim. The felt band of the black Stetson was impaled with a collection of dry flies and fishhooks.

"Fred Bolte," Troy muttered aloud, and slid his gun into leather. "You've done your last fishin' this side of hell, *hombre.*"

Identifying one of his ambushers as Bix Herrod's personal bodyguard removed the last mystery behind the destruction of his mules and wagon tonight. Herrod, learning through some source—perhaps from Shasta Ives—that the man who blocked his summer range was making a trek to Coulee City, had dispatched two of his Lazy H gunhawks to wait for him here at Dry Falls, knowing it was the only means of crossing Grand Coulee from the Indian Reservation.

For the first time since the strike of lead against his own flesh, Troy realized now the seriousness of what Herrod's men had accomplished tonight. His best wagon and the pick of his mules were now buzzard bait and kindling wood in the pit of the Lower Coulee. Herrod had made a second strike at Troy's source of livelihood, augmenting this blow with a direct try on Troy's life.

If Troy had had any doubts as to the limit Herrod would go, this business at Dry Falls removed them. The chips were down in a game which had a boothill grave waiting for one or both of them at its finish.

Troy clambered back down to the ledge and recovered his Winchester and Stetson. Back on the rise where Fred Bolte's sightless eyes stared at the weltering moon, the Texan wrestled briefly with a vindictive impulse to hurl the Lazy H bodyguard over the rim.

Instead he picked up Bolte's fishhook-bristling sombrero and, shouldering his rifle infantry fashion, headed toward the lights of Coulee City, five miles by

49

crowflight across the desert. The coyotes could quarrel over Bolte's corpse tonight; Troy knew that getting medical attention for his wound was his first need.

If he remembered correctly, there would be a stage leaving Coulee City for the Okanogan country around noon tomorrow, He would board it, with a dead man's hat as his only extra baggage.

CHAPTER SEVEN

A DEAD MAN'S HAT

CATTLE BEARING THE LAZY H AND DOLLAR brands and earmarks plodded up the cliff-bordered bottoms of the Columbia River, ribby and gaunted from a hard winter and a burned-out spring.

Bracketed by yipping outriders, Bix Herrod's pool herd was strung out in a dusty column which measured five miles from its point to the drags.

Behind them lay the parched Ellensburg hills, the river settlements of Rock Island and Wenatchee. Directly ahead was the cluster of shacks marking Entiat.

The majority of these three thousand head of bawling cattle belonged to Bix Herrod; the remainder were Sam Ives's legacy to his daughter, and a smattering of mavericks, picked up en route through the Colokum Pass by Herrod's hungry-looped drovers.

Herrod was waiting for his herd's arrival when they forded Entiat River. With the unerring instinct of a stockman, he saw that the pool herd was beginning to take on tallow during its leisurely advance northward, and grass improved from here on.

Paced by a chuck wagon, the herd was within a

hundred miles of its summer range at Flaming Canyon now. Riding out to confer with his trail boss, Herrod left orders to favor the stragglers, nurse the she-stuff along, take it easy.

He had plenty of time. A few months on the lush grass of the Okanogan would put Lazy H and Dollar beef in shape for the fall gather and the short drive through Snoqualmie Pass to the slaughterhouses in Seattle. And with the Yakima and Oregon ranges ruined by drought this year, Herrod stood to rake in a fat profit on a beef-short market. The feed and water of Flaming Canyon would guarantee that.

Turning back up the Cariboo Trail toward the Okanogan, Herrod rode with a vast contentment suffusing him, a welcome release after the strain of past months, when he had seen his fortunes shriveling under the tropical hot Washington sun.

A proud, ruthless, and thoroughly unscrupulous cattleman, Bix Herrod's sleep was not deviled by so much as a shred of worry concerning the end of this cattle drive. He rode with the firm assurance that the temporary nuisance of Del Troy's presence at Flaming Canyon would be disposed of long in advance of the herd's arrival at the homesteader's drift fence.

He had known Troy casually, as a happy-go-lucky saddle bum back in Texas, a decade ago. It had come as a surprise to find that the erstwhile Chisholm Trail drifter had acquired ambitions to build a spread of his own out here in Washington.

But Herrod was quick to see that Troy's scheme to introduce big-scale Texas methods of cattle raising to the unsettled Okanogan had possibilities which he, Herrod might well adapt to his own long-range objective of dominating the cattle industry of this

51

northwestern frontier.

Whereas Herrod owned leagues of rich cattle range in the Yakima country, he had savvy enough to foresee other rainless years such as this one. If, by gaining title to permanent summer range in Flaming Canyon, he could assure the prosperity of his cattle empire, Herrod was prepared to take any steps to wipe out any opposition which might confront his greedy ambition.

Shasta Ives figured in that ambition. When Herrod had first arrived in Washington, well heeled with the proceeds of his crooked loop and running-iron back in Texas, his only neighbor had been aging Sam Ives, one-time brevet colonel under Jeb Stuart.

Ives, coming to Washington Territory shortly after the humiliation at Appomattox, had founded the Dollar ranch, married, and begot a daughter, whom he had named after the snow-clad peak which overshadowed his wife's home in California.

Colonel Sam had looked with distrust upon Bix Herrod, fearful of how far his fellow Texan's shadow might fall. He had seen Herrod build up the vast Lazy H outfit, freezing out small-tally ranchers with the aid of the gun-hung crew he had brought with him from the Lone Star plains.

Ives had died last winter, thereby removing the last obstacle to Herrod's long-range scheme to monopolize the privately owned grazing range in the State of Washington. Shasta Ives was twenty years younger than Herrod, but he had courted her with an ardent devotion which had slowly overcome her father's opposition to the match.

Only on the death of old Sam, in his ninetieth year, had the girl finally consented to wear Herrod's ring; and then with a patent reluctance which had piqued Herrod's pride. To Herrod, such a marriage was based less on love than on more practical business grounds. Once Shasta became his bride, the Dollar would automatically fall into the sphere of control which the Lazy H wielded in the Yakima country.

A man of unquestionable social charm and education, Bix Herrod chose to consider his forthcoming marriage to Shasta Ives as icing on a very delectable cake. The rambling California-style ranch house which Herrod had built on a tawny bluff overlooking his cattle empire needed a hostess. And Shasta's beauty made her a prize well worth capturing, even without the added inducement of Dollar's fertile acres of Natchez Valley graze.

As Shasta's intended husband, Herrod knew he enjoyed the girl's complete faith and unswerving loyalty. His personal integrity was something she had never questioned, despite the hints which Colonel Sam had implanted in her regarding Herrod's rustling activities back in Texas.

However Herrod had managed to expand his range, Shasta accepted his version of astute business dealings and fair payment for value received. Stories of night raids by Lazy H riders, small-tally ranchers left dangling under cottonwood limbs as the price of their defiance to Lazy H and its spreading power—these stories Herrod could pass off as ugly rumors started by jealous inferiors. And, knowing Shasta's deep-seated inheritance of honor and square dealing, Herrod was careful to curry the girl's respect in every way he could.

Midway to Brewster, where Herrod intended to await his oncoming pool herd, the Lazy H cattle baron was hailed from the shadow of the beetling Ribbon Cliffs by a familiar voice.

Reining his big stallion in the direction of the voice, Herrod saw the familiar sunken-chested figure of Doc Godette emerge from a willow thicket at the river's edge.

Excitement put a flush of color on Herrod's cheekbones as he spurred down to meet his henchman. Exactly where his path had first crossed Godette's, even Herrod could not remember precisely, but a close rapport had always existed between this ambitious wide-looper and the broken-down, ex-Confederate surgeon.

Crowding seventy, Doc Godette had been a practicing physician in an obscure Texas trail town during the reconstruction years that followed his mustering out from the Confederate forces. But drink and opium had made Godette a pariah of his profession, a traitor to his Hippocratic Oath.

His habit of administering to patients who visited him in the dead of night, owlhooters with a bounty on their scalps and gunshot or knife wounds of doubtful genesis on their persons, had given Mike Godette a notoriety and a crooked reputation.

At any rate, the oldster's genius with scalpel and suture needle had saved Bix Herrod's life on a certain occasion when a Texas Ranger had put a bullet in Herrod's lung following an unsuccessful attempt to steal a herd bound for Abilene.

Godette, in the early stages of tuberculosis even then, had carried the wounded rustler to Medora and devoted the next six months of his life to concealing Herrod from the posses seeking to cut his sign, and had nursed Herrod through a convalescence when another medico would have given up his patient as lost.

As long as that bullet scar remained on Herrod's chest, he owed an unshakable allegiance to Doc

Godette, the only loyalty that the man was capable of. And on that basis their Damon and Pythias relationship had its inception.

When Herrod had come West to shake off the law noose that was tightening around him in the brasada country of the upper Pecos, Bix Herrod's companion in flight had been Doc Godette; and with the ascending star of Lazy H fortune, Godette carried the title of Herrod's foreman and was his inseparable companion and personal adviser.

"You killed Troy?" Herrod greeted the rawboned old man.

Godette shielded a cough behind a palsied palm and when he lowered his hand, a stain of crimson lingered on the corners of his mouth. His forearm was pitted with hypodermic scars and his faded eyes were pinpointed with narcotics now.

"Well, Bix, I'll answer that one with a yes or no."

Herrod swung out of stirrups, his flat brows jutting like awnings over his narrowing eyes.

"What in hell does that mean, yes or no? He's either dead or he damned better had be." Herrod's piercing flint-black eyes lanced through the willows behind Godette. "Where's Fred?"

Godette rubbed the worn stock of his ancient Spiller and Burr campaign pistol, avoiding Herrod's glance.

"I left Bolte back at the Dry Falls. We jumped Troy's wagon, set it afire, and hazed it over the cliff. But Fred got careless. Forgot there was a full moon. Troy blew his brains out."

Herrod pulled his bridle reins back and forth through his powerful hands, his jaw sagging as he took the brunt of this shocking news. Fred Bolte had sided Herrod for years before Godette had joined the triumvirate. He and

55

Bolte had shot their way out of more than one tight corner together, back to back.

"What happened to Troy?"

Godette's interest appeared to be fixed on the black lava seams that laced the eroded face of the Ribbon Cliffs overhead.

"Well, Bolte plugged him. Troy forted up in the rocks and I reckon he bled to death there."

A grim prescience of disaster flowed through Herrod. "Out with it, Doc. It ain't like you to beat around the bush with me. You ain't sure Troy cashed in his chips?"

Godette fished a bottle from his tunic and fortified himself with a stiff dram. Having long since diagnosed his own incurable disease, Godette kept himself alive with alcohol and morphine.

"I lit a shuck soon as I found Bolte was past my help, Bix. I'd say Troy bled to death, but I didn't dally around till daylight to make sure. I'm too old a goat to risk my horns with a younker."

Herrod was silent for a long interval, his knuckles whitening over the stocks of the twin Colts slung for cross draw under his fustian town coat.

"I should have handled Troy myself," he said finally. "Get your bronc and come on, Doc. We'll eat at Brewster."

Dusk found Herrod and Godette at the ferry landing opposite Fort Columbia. The Ribbon Cliffs, forcing a closure of the Cariboo Trail, meant the oncoming herd would have to cross to the east bank of the Columbia. By noon tomorrow the cattle would reach Port Columbia and make their crossing back to the west side where the river was narrowest.

Guerrant's ferry cables had been repaired and the raft, towed back upstream from the bar where it had landed with Troy's wagon, was once more in operation. At the moment it was shuttling back to Brewster, loaded with the red-and-yellow stage from Wilbur and Coulee City.

When the ferry nudged into its slip, the stage driver mounted his boot and drove the thoroughbraced Concord up the ramp and halted in front of the Brewster station, directly opposite Guerrant's shanty.

Herrod, his chair tilted back against the wall of the ferryman's house, was dozing when Doc Godette plucked his sleeve.

"Reckon my diagnosis of Troy's wound was a trifle on the optimistic side, Bix. Look a-comin' yonder and remember you left your shootin'-irons in your alforja bags."

The color drained from Herrod's swart countenance as he caught sight of the tall, bowlegged cowpuncher who alighted from the Coulee City stage and headed toward the ferry landing.

Del Troy halted in front of Herrod, his smoke-gray eyes shuttling between Doc Godette and the Lazy H boss. His left hand came out from behind his back and he tossed a black sombrero on the step at Herrod's feet.

"See you at Flaming Canyon next week, Bix. Meanwhile, there's a little keepsake for you in case you want to go fishin'."

So saying, the Texan turned on his heel and strode back to catch the departing stage for Conconully.

"Fred's skypiece," Doc Godette muttered, staring at the bullet hole in the brim of the bloodstained sombrero. "Well, Troy knows what he's up against, anyhow. He doesn't know I was with Fred that night or I wouldn't be here to brag about it now."

57

CHAPTER EIGHT

"MY WORD AGAINST TROY'S"

AMBIE PRIDE, THE BROKEN-DOWN PROSPECTOR WHO enjoyed the dubious distinction of being Conconully's town drunkard, was on hand at the relay station when the midnight stage pulled in from Brewster.

A lone passenger alighted from the Concord, and Ambie Pride hobbled over to make his customary plea.

"I'm dead beat for nourishment an' you can't eat free lunch at Beagle's Saloon without buyin' a drink, stranger. Besides which my wife Jennie is fixin' to have a baby an' I'm needing a bracer."

Pride's whimper broke off as he recognized the drawn lines of Del Troy's face in the glare of the stage lamps. Ordinarily the genial Texan was good for a dollar and a few joshing words, but tonight Troy brushed off the beggar's outstretched palm and stalked grimly across the street to Slankard & Company's office.

He found the bearded trader playing checkers with Irv Gaddy, the sheriff. After a moment's hesitation, Troy decided to let the lawman in on his failure to reach Coulee City to pick up Slankard's merchandise.

". . . Herrod's cattle are bedded down this side of Pateros tonight," he finished up. "Which means they'll hit my Flaming Canyon fence in two or three days at the outside. I can't make the Coulee trip with my other wagon or send Whitey over there either, Steen."

The trader fingered his beard thoughtfully.

"No matter. I'd just have that much more inventory I couldn't dispose of. Sorry you lost your outfit, son. Never rains but it pours, seems like."

Sheriff Gaddy, apparently concentrating on his next move, rubbed a leaf-brown ear and spoke through his drooping waterfall mustache.

"If you can prove Bix Herrod was behind that ambush, swear out a warrant for his arrest and I'll he glad to serve it, Del. If somebody don't put a rope around that guy's neck he'll be running for gov'nor."

Troy, his hand on the doorknob, shook his head in negation. "Bolte's dead. I didn't identify his partner. Herrod was behind the deal, obviously. But proving it is something else."

Troy stepped out into the night, saw that the Loop-Loop Casino was locked up—an unheard-of thing for a gambling-house which did its best business in the hours after midnight—and, after a yearning glance at the window of Roxanna's upstairs bedroom, made his way to the Cariboo House.

Sheriff Gaddy was breakfasting in the hotel dining-room when Troy joined him next morning, refreshed after a good sleep. He was wearing a clean shirt which concealed the lump of bandage taped to his left shoulder.

Gaddy waited until Troy was building a smoke after his meal before saying what was on his mind.

"Del, I was talking to Ambie Pride after I seen you last night. Had to lock the old coot up to sleep off a binge. It seems Ambie has been on a huntin' trip over Flaming Canyon way."

Troy grinned at the picture that conjured up. "Aiming to feed that new baby a venison steak when the stork shows up?"

Gaddy's face was dead serious as he teetered back his chair, furbishing the star on his gallus strap with a horny thumb.

"You know that section of public land between your homesteads and the Twenty-Mile Strip?"

"At Keyhole Pass? I ought to, Irv. Been trying hard enough to get you or some other reliable person to prove up on it, to protect my back. Don't tell me Ambie Pride wants to file on it!"

Gaddy scratched a stubbly jaw with his pipestem.

"Not hardly. But Ambie Pride says somebody's fencin' that piece and is throwin' up a homestead cabin smack in the middle of the Keyhole. It wouldn't be so good, say, if Bix Herrod got the idea of taking a donation claim right at your back door."

Troy's chair legs hit the floor as he came to his feet. The Keyhole had always been the weak link in his plan to eventually control the entire length of Flaming Canyon. If a hostile owner moved in, he could legally demand right-of-way between Troy's and Whitey Crade's homestead, through the mouth of the Canyon. That possibility had long been a nightmare to the man.

"The courthouse opens in a couple hours," the sheriff went on, a toothpick waggling under his mustache. "Dazzy Kline can tell you soon enough who filed the claim on Keyhole."

Troy lifted his Stetson from a near-by antler rack. "Hell, I can be out to the Canyon by then. I'll find out for myself."

Troy was saddling his steelduster over in Slankard's barn before the Conconully sheriff caught up with him.

"I'll ride out with you, son. You might find a gent with an itchy trigger finger squattin' on that section."

Troy jerked his latigo tight and mounted. "No, thanks, sheriff. Filing on an unclaimed chunk of government land is nothing a sheriff can object to."

"Of course," Gaddy called after him, "this whole

60

thing might be another of Pride's whisky tales."

The steelduster was lathered and blowing when Troy reached the south wall of Flaming Canyon and directed his gaze toward the narrowing notch of the Keyhole.

Ambie Pride's report had been no figment of a drunkard's imagination. A pile of notched fir logs had been snaked over to the Keyhole. Two men were already at work, even at this early hour, fashioning a foundation from rocks brought from the bed of Glacier Creek. And a row of fence posts had been set across the section line. Reels of barbed wire gleamed in the morning sunrays from the bed of a springboard wagon parked near the creek. Wire purchased from Slankard's stock.

And Troy made another grim discovery. The nesters he was depending upon to harvest his hay crop were nowhere to be seen—their tents were gone and their rakes and mowing machines were nowhere in evidence. The sodbusters had deserted the sinking ship during his absence.

Troy spurred his winded mustang recklessly down the road which ribboned down the shoulder of the canyon, and reached his own homestead. The anguished bawling of his milk cow pulled Troy's attention from the Keyhole situation, and he tarried to pay his log-walled barn a visit.

The cow's udder was swollen with pent-up milk, indicative that Whitey Crade had been derelict in his duty to the suffering animal during Troy's absence. Cursing, the Texan wasted a quarter hour stripping the cow, pumping the water trough full, and forking fresh hay to the neglected beast.

Back in saddle, he skirted his cabin and was swinging across the flats in the direction of the new homestead claim at the Keyhole when a scene of activity over on his partner's homestead brought him up short, his original mission pushed from his mind.

A crew of men was strung out along Crade's drift fence, cutting barbed wire and yanking posts out of the ground with lass' ropes. The barrier which Troy had counted upon to indicate the deadline for Herrod's pool herd was being obliterated before his very eyes.

Loosening his saddle gun in scabbard, Troy put the steelduster at a dead run across the intervening flats, forded Glacier Creek, and reined up in front of Whitey Crade's tarpaper shack.

"Whitey!" his bellow started echoes from the looming cliff. "What in hell have you b—"

He broke off, as the cabin door opened on bullhide hinges and the trim figure of Shasta Ives stepped out on the clean-swept stone flags of his partner's porch.

The girl from Dollar was hatless, the sun catching highlights in her cascading blond tresses. She looked mannish in a pair of high-cuffed bibless Levis, and her shirt sleeves were rolled back to reveal arms whitened with baking-powder.

Ground-tying the steelduster, Troy headed for the house, a storm of conflicting emotions keeping him speechless even when the girl gave him a cordial invitation to join her at breakfast.

"Where's my partner?" he blurted finally.

Devils danced in Shasta's brown eyes. "Mr. Crade is staying over in Conconully until you return, I believe he said."

Troy gestured toward the drift fence. "Who's that out yonder tearing down fence? What are you doing here at Crade's?"

Shasta swatted her palms together, flour clouding up to obscure her half-smile.

"Those are Dollar cowhands, Mr. Troy. They work for me. I own this homestead, as of Wednesday noon."

"You—" Troy swayed on his feet, unable to comprehend this cataclysmic turn of events. "I never called a woman a liar, ma'am, but Crade wouldn't sell me down the river. Not without consulting me first."

Shasta leaned back against the door casing, folding her arms across the swell of her breasts.

"I'm sorry, Mr. Troy, but you're mistaken. Mr. Crade sold me this homestead the day you left for Coulee City. For a thousand dollars in cash. Do you want to see my deed?"

Knots of muscle swelled at the corners of Troy's jaws as a deep, festering hurt took root in his breast. The ambush at Dry Falls, this stab in the back over at the Keyhole today, even the threat of imminent range war which Bix Herrod's approaching cattle presaged—these calamities were tangible, something a man could fight in his own way.

But to have a trusted partner play the Judas role in his absence—to be double-crossed by a man who owed Troy his life, his one chance of salvaging his manhood—this was a tragedy too deep to absorb at one blow.

"Please don't look at me that way, Mr. Troy," Shasta implored, her arrogance fading as she stepped toward him. "After all, everything's fair in love and war. And this is surely war between us. My whole future is tied up in gaining right-of-way for my stock to enter Flaming Canyon. Mr. Crade is not your slave or your chattel. He had a perfect legal and moral right to accept cash payment for property he held in his own right."

Troy's lungs expanded to the slow, deep pull of his breath, his face ashen as the face of a pugilist who has sustained a crippling blow, his brain as yet incapable of realizing the potentialities of disaster which Crade's perfidy would bring.

"Yeah," he said numbly, "everything's fair in love and war. Even to tipping off a killer that I'd be prime ambush bait out at Grand Coulee, I suppose!"

A frown altered the girl's face, pulling the anger from her eyes. She drew back her hand in the act of touching him. "Grand Coulee? Ambush? What are you talking about?"

He laughed then, harshly and on a rising scale. His hands fisted, every instinct in him calling out for physical reprisal, his rage checkmated by the barrier of sex.

"Don't lie to me! Don't deny you sent Fred Bolte out to ambush me! Well, I had to kill Fred Bolte. The first life I ever took. You can laugh and forget that. I never will."

Shasta recoiled from the ferocity of his eyes, seeing a berserk quality enter his uncurbed temper.

"I know nothing of Bolte's activities," she said hollowly. "Surely you don't think I—I'd condone anything as violent as—"

He was gone then, striding back to his waiting horse. He swung into stirrups and left Crade's gate at a run.

For a long minute the girl remained at the cabin door, a sense of shame touching her, a feeling akin to disloyalty to her better self that erased what triumph she had felt at engineering a tactical victory over this homesteader she felt to be an enemy.

The strike of hoofs approaching from the east drew her gaze away from Del Troy's departure toward Keyhole Pass. Shasta pulled her gaze around to see Bix Herrod riding through the gate from the direction of the fence-cutting crew.

"It worked, Shasta!" the Lazy H boss shouted

64

exultantly as he stepped down from his stallion. "I thought Crade would be putty in your hands, but I hardly expected to find a hundred-and-sixty-acre gate wide open before I got back."

She evaded his attempt to kiss her, and not until then did Bix Herrod pause to see the haunted look in his fiancée's eyes.

"Shasta, honey! What's troubling you this morning?"

Shasta stepped back, her eyes imploring him. "Bix, tell me the truth. What happened to Fred Bolte?"

Herrod's smile faded, his eyes shuttering as if to conceal the guilty knowledge that lay behind them.

"What do you mean?"

"Troy was just here. He says Fred tried to ambush him over at Grand Coulee night before last. He says he had to shoot Fred."

Herrod's jaw snapped shut. He stalled for time to compose his thoughts by clipping the end off his cigar and lighting it.

"Matter of fact, Bolte is dead," he admitted. "I sent him back down to meet the herd, as you know. He got himself knifed by a jezebel down in Wenatchee's red-light district Saturday night. Doc brought me the news at Pateros. I helped bury Fred yesterday."

Tears brimmed the girl's lashes as she stared back at the man she intended to marry, a tiny worm of disillusion screwing into her thoughts for the first time since she had accepted Herrod's betrothal ring.

"Bix—you wouldn't lie to me—about Fred?"

Herrod was smiling again now, his arms extended toward her. A moment later she was pressed against him, sobbing uncontrollably against his lapel.

"Of course I told you the truth, Shasta. It's my word against Troy's. Which of us are you to believe?"

CHAPTER NINE

A CRAZE TO KILL

THE TWO BURLY STONE MASONS WHO WERE LAYING the foundation for the Keyhole Pass cabin paused in their work as Troy rode up. He recalled having seen this pair around Conconully before, and had the impression that they were muckers at the Silver King diggings.

"Which one of you filed on this land?"

The workmen exchanged glances, sensing the threat in the horsebacker's voice.

"Neither of us, feller. We just took on this fencin' and cabin-raisin' job to kill time while the mine's closed down. Got the job from Nick Jordano, the shafthouse foreman."

"Since when is a mining engineer interested in a homestead? There's no mineral in Flaming Canyon. It's been prospected from end to end. Jordano knows that."

The spokesman shrugged. "Jordano didn't file on it. Somebody braced him for day labor and he give us the job. That's all we can tell you."

There was nothing to be gained by dallying here. Troy wheeled the steelduster around and started back to town.

The county courthouse was open when Troy reached Conconully and he went directly to the land office. Dazzy Kline, the county recorder, was going through his morning mail.

"I'd like to see your plat of Flaming Canyon," Troy requested brusquely, without preliminaries. "Want to find out who filed on that public land near the Keyhole this week."

66

Kline cuffed back the celluloid eyeshade which cowled his bald head and grinned competently.

"No need to open the archives for that dope, Troy. Your lady friend over at the Loop-Loop took a notion to be your neighbor."

Troy's jaw dropped. "Meaning Roxanna Laranjo?"

"That's right. Gamblin's dead around here. Maybe she wants to settle down and grow garden truck."

Troy left the courthouse in a haze of relief and bewilderment. Not until he was hitching his mustang at the rack in front of the Loop-Loop deadfall did the full import of Roxie's surprise move become clear to him: *She heard about Crade selling me out, so she filed on the Keyhole. With Roxie homesteadin' that piece, Herrod can't shove a single critter beyond her boundary fence.*

The implications of the girl's coup buoyed Troy's spirit like a narcotic in his bloodstream. Between the Lazy H herd and the upper Canyon, Roxanna's homestead stood like a barrier as effective as if an avalanche had blocked the Keyhole. There could be no other explanation for the girl's move. In his absence, she had countered Whitey Crade's treachery with a master stroke, plucking victory from what had seemed irrevocable defeat.

Troy mounted the Casino steps and pushed through the batwings, his eyes sweeping at once to the blackjack table in the far corner. He was in luck. Roxanna, wearing a full-skirted Spanish gown that made her resemble a damosela from old Castile, was fitting a new baize cover to her gaming-table.

A lone customer stood drinking at the Casino's bar, standing in Troy's path as the Texan headed toward Roxanna's corner Not until he was abreast of the man did he recognize Whitey Crade, and sight of his traitorous partner halted Troy alongside Crade's elbow.

On the bar in front of the albino was a half-empty whisky bottle, a shot glass, and a buckskin poke from the puckered mouth of which had spilled a heap of gold specie.

"Spending your double-cross pay on forty-rod, Whitey?" Troy's voice cut through Crade's alcoholic fog. "How do you think you'll feel when that dinero's gone and you have to live with yourself?"

Crade clutched the plump leather sack with trembling hands, swiveling slowly to meet the full impact of Troy's scorn. His obscene, corpse-white face took on two spots of color over his cheekbones as he tried to focus his pink eyes on the man he had betrayed to the enemy.

"I had a right to sell out, Del. Who in hell do you think you are—my guardeen?"

Crade's voice was thick with whisky. His side-hammer .36 pistol was thrust under his belt and his ruby-dark eyes were bright with a malevolent defiance.

A sneer plucked at the corners of Troy's mouth. "Sure," his reply came gently. "You had a right to sell out. The homestead belonged to you. You owed me nothing. Forget it."

Crade lurched away from the bar as Troy started toward Roxanna again. The albino jerked the drawstring of the gold poke taut and spun it on a forefinger.

"I'll split the dinero with you, Del. You damned bastard, take it all. Here—catch!"

As he spoke, Whitey Crade tossed the bag of specie in a looping arc toward Troy's face, in a feint to mask his simultaneous reach for the five-shot revolver at his hip.

Reading the trick even as it came, Troy parried the leather pouch in mid-air, batting it back against the albino's chest and following up with a pounce which caught Crade's gun arm on its upward jerk from his belt.

They grappled, Crade's left knee battering at Troy's crotch as they struggled for possession of the gun. A hard twist of both hands on Crade's wrist brought a bellow of pain from the albino, and the unfired Root .36 dropped into a sand box beside the brass rail between them.

Crade wrenched himself free of Troy's traplike grip and scooped the whisky bottle off the bar. Troy ducked under the swinging bottle, felt it graze the bullet wound on his shoulder with an impact that shot fire through his vitals.

The bottle left Crade's grasp and splintered on the floor behind them. The bartender's nervous yell was lost on Troy's ears. "Gentlemen! Gentlemen! I'll tolerate no violence in this house. Take your argument outdoors."

Troy rocked Crade back on his heels with a blow to the nose which brought crimson spewing from the albino's nostrils. Stepping wide, Troy unbuckled his gun harness and flung it on the bar, his eyes never leaving Crade.

"We can settle our accounts without gunplay, Whitey. Come on."

All reason had left Crade's liquor-fuddled brain now. He lunged at his former partner with fists flailing, the craze to kill blazing in his red-shot eyes, curses spilling from twisted lips.

Crade's frenzied assault drove Troy back against a poker table, upsetting it with a dry clatter of spilling chips and a crumbling chair. Troy lost his footing on the puddle of spilled whisky behind him and he went down, powerless to dodge Crade's out-lashing boot.

69

The kick grazed his jaw, snapping his head back. Through a red gauze of pain he saw the albino leaping for him, butchering his flesh with kicks and blows as Crade pulled the fight to the level of a saloon brawl, kicking, gouging, no holds barred.

Troy rolled free and came to his feet, snatching up a croupier's stool from the roulette layout and beating it over Crade's shoulders. But still the albino bored in, murderous, bawling deep in his throat like a wounded bull after a matador, driven by an insane passion to stomp the life from the man who faced him, a powerful maniac whose strength was doubled by the drunken fury which possessed him.

The batwings flashed open and revealed the crouched figure of Sheriff Gaddy on the threshold, as the two fighters slugged their way in a serpentine path through the rows of gaming-tables.

Roxie Laranjo's passage was a breath of perfume and a rustle of silk as the girl fled across the barroom to where the sheriff stood, hand on gun butt, bitter lights in his eyes.

"Stop them, Irv—oh, in God's name, stop them before they kill each other."

Gaddy shook his head, watched Troy chop Crade's face to a bloody ruin as they smashed each other toe to toe in the middle of the Casino, men evenly matched for weight and reach and a mutual determination to make this a finish fight, the swan song of their broken partnership.

"Crade sold Troy out," Gaddy said mercilessly. "Less'n the rabbit-eyed freak tries pulling any Injun tricks, I'll let Troy dish out the medicine Crade's got coming to him."

Roxanna averted her eyes as the fury of battle carried

Troy and Crade against the bar with a resounding crash, trading uppercuts with a furious abandon which brought no pain to either man.

Crade retreated along the bar, tiring fast. He stooped once to seize up a brass cuspidor and hurled it, screaming, at the bruised visage of the Texan who followed him relentlessly, carrying the fight to him. Troy ducked the hurtling bludgeon and leaped to block Crade's possible retreat toward a side door, fists lancing through the albino's defenses to pound Crade's lips to a jelly and bruise the albino's chest and stomach with a merciless rain of blows.

Sheriff Gaddy pulled Roxanna clear of the doorway as the brawling pair veered away from the end of the bar and hit the batwings, locked in a grapple. They crashed heavily to the porch outside and Crade was the first on his feet, stomping Troy's skull and back with spike-heel boots.

Gaddy followed them through the fanning doors, gun half drawn as he saw Crade's bloody fingers lock on Troy's throat, thumbs probing for the windpipe, his sunflower rowels raking Troy's flanks and thighs, slashing Troy's bullhide chaps to ribbons.

Troy broke the strangling grip on his neck and reared to his feet, smashing a haymaker to Crade's solar plexus which carried the albino backward to hit a porch post with splintering impact.

Recovering, Crade's fist stabbed to his belt and sunlight flashed on naked steel as the albino got a bowie blade from its sheath under his Levis.

The sheriff's gun was in the open now, but before the lawman could intervene Troy had launched himself under Crade's thrusting knife and his head caught the albino in the short ribs, butting him in a backward somersault over the Casino's porch rail.

71

The knife clattered out on the plank sidewalk as Whitey Crade collapsed moaning in the weeds alongside the porch. He was whipped, utterly spent. Troy, his shirt hanging in rags about his heaving chest, stumbled down the steps and reached down to grab his erstwhile partner by the armpits, hauling him to his feet.

"Your horse is at the rack, Whitey," Troy's voice gusted like a crow's caw from his laboring throat. "Straddle it and ride. There ain't room in the Okanogans for the two of us after today."

Mopping blood from his eyes with a ragged sleeve, Whitey Crade lurched dazedly across the sidewalk and clutched the end of the hitchrack for support, blood dripping in gobbets from his crushed nose and mouth to stipple the dirt, his head bowed on his chest.

Crade was beyond speech or movement when the Casino's trembling bartender came outside with the albino's gold poke and gun. Sheriff Gaddy seized the latter, emptied the loads from the cylinder, and walked over to thrust the empty gun into Crade's hip pocket.

"You heard what Troy said," the sheriff rasped out. "Hit the trail, Whitey. And keep going. I'll lock you up for life if I ketch you inside my county again."

It took the combined efforts of Gaddy and the bartender to hoist Crade aboard his claybank gelding. Sagging in saddle as if his spine were broken, Crade stared around dizzily while the bartender stowed Shasta Ives's gold into a saddlebag.

Fumbling with his reins, Crade peered through swollen lids, hunting until he located Del Troy leaning against a porch post, gasping air into his tortured lungs.

"I'm pullin' stakes," croaked the albino. "But fog your guns next time our trails cross. I ain't forgettin' this, damn your black soul. Not ever."

72

Clinging to saddle horn, Crade spurred away from the Casino and headed the gelding down-canyon toward the Ruby diggings. Sheriff Gaddy crossed over to the porch of the Silver Exchange Bank and posted himself in a rocker there, keeping an eye on Crade until the banished albino was lost behind the pines at the south end of town, headed into exile.

Roxanna materialized at Troy's side when the Texan brought himself groggily out of torpor, his eyes bleak with disillusion that allowed no trace of exultation over this hard-won brawl.

"Breaking a friendship isn't easy, Del," the girl's whisper reached his throbbing ears. "Don't let Whitey's parting threat bother you, *querido.* He won't stop riding till he gets back to Texas where he belongs, that I know."

Troy lowered his eyes to meet the message of faith and pride he read in Roxanna's somber gaze, and for the first time he recalled the reason that had sent him into the gambling-house.

"I wanted to thank you for making that Keyhole deal for me, Roxie," he said huskily, words coming hard. "Herrod would have had me hogtied for branding if you hadn't moved in to scotch his play."

She pulled his head to her and kissed him once, lightly and impersonally on his bruised cheek, and old hungers swept Troy again as he rubbed his aching jaw against her glossy raven hair, holding her thus for a long moment.

"I had my reasons, Del," she told him, and he felt her withdraw behind the mantle of aloof mystery which would forever be a barrier between them.

CHAPTER TEN

OUT OF THE FRYING-PAN—

DUST ROILED UP FROM THE CARIBOO TRAIL AS THE Lazy H and Dollar pool herd approached the fruit orchards of the nesters around Omak Ford. It was a dust that built a curtain across the zenith and turned the sun to a copper rivet, tempering the unseasonable heat which was slowly turning the foothill forests into a tinderbox.

Farmers watched the sprawled brown tidal wave of hoofs and horns approach their unfenced apple orchards and were apprehensive of what Bix Herrod's drovers would do when they reached the outer limits of the plowed and planted bottomlands.

At a community meeting two days before the sodbusters had voted, reluctantly but in solid majority, to abandon their haying contract with Del Troy. The level heads among them, veterans of cattle wars in other places, knew the potential battleground which Flaming Canyon had become. Hints of the Lazy H's violent methods of expanding its cattle empire had trickled up the trail from Yakima, and these nesters had no stomach for hang-rope or raiders' torches by night.

It was with relief then, that they saw the oncoming herd quit the greening riverbottom and move into the eroded coulees which serrated the lofty tableland that formed a buffer between the pine-mottled foot spurs of the Cascades and the river valley.

For the nesters, the emergency was at least postponed, and there were few among them who believed that a lone cowman like Del Troy could long stand against the

74

pressure of Herrod's cloven-hoofed juggernaut.

Throughout the sweltering day, Yakima riders hazed the bawling stragglers up the claybanked brakes, bunching the herd on the grassy bench of Pogue's Flat. A mile due west of this bedground, the frowning obsidian ramparts of the Cascade Range were broken by the broad, inviting maw of Flaming Canyon, its remoter extremity pointing like a crooked finger into the snow-watered Eden of the high hills where the drought had not yet penetrated.

It was too late in the day to push the herd into the Canyon, but Bix Herrod had learned of minor formalities to get out of the way before the vanguard of the beef drive started its entry onto long-awaited summer range.

Shasta Ives, who had moved out from the Conconully Hotel to live on the Crade homestead for the summer, had informed Herrod of the barbed-wire fence which had mysteriously been strung across the narrowing hourglass formation of the Canyon, at Keyhole Pass.

That fence had been completed secretly during the week, connecting up with the back line of Del Troy's homestead on the south half of the canyon mouth. It formed an unbroken barrier from cliff to cliff. duplicating the fence which Dollar cowhands had removed from Crade's frontage in advance of the herd's arrival.

As evening's blue dusk was pooling between the rimrocks, Herrod rode toward the Keyhole with Shasta Ives and the ubiquitous segundo, Doc Godette, flanking his stirrups. Herrod scorned to make any show of force by bringing an armed crew with him. Whoever had dared file on the homestead rights to the Keyhole was obviously in ignorance of the powderkeg he had chosen for a claim.

75

The walls and rafters of the new homestead cabin had been raised between Glacier Creek and the Keyhole notch, fifty yards from the triple strands of barbed wire which closed Flaming Canyon to the cattle herd bedded down on the outer flats tonight.

As the three riders drew rein at the wire gate, Herrod's halloo brought two men and a girl from the doorless and windowless cabin. Herrod recognized their sharp-cut silhouettes against the red wash of sundown glow through the Keyhole, and sight of them brought him erect in saddle.

"What's Roxie Laranjo doing here?" he exclaimed, as if to himself. And his eyes were on Del Troy and the Conconully sheriff, Irv Gaddy.

Shasta bent a curious stare at her fiancé. "She's the lady gambler at the Loop-Loop Casino, isn't she? You've met her before, Bix?"

Doc Godette, preoccupied with a whisky bottle to ease off the pains of a recent coughing spell, did not fail to notice the quick alarm which clouded Herrod's eyes as Shasta spoke.

"She used to dance in a honkytonk in San Antone, Shasta. Everybody west of the Pecos knows Roxie Laranjo."

Del Troy and the sheriff dropped slightly behind the dusky-eyed Spanish girl as she reached the fence, her gaze striking Herrod with a blinkless intensity, her carmine lips parted in an inscrutable smile, alike hostile and provocative.

"Evenin', Roxie," Herrod said, lifting his Keevil hat. "What are you doing here?"

Strange and obscure cross currents flowed between this pair for a moment. Then Roxanna shifted her attention to Shasta Ives, her glance carrying on to Doc

76

Godette, who sat his horse with the silence of a graven image, shrouded in his own thoughts, knowing more than his poker face revealed.

"This is my homestead, Señor Herrod," Roxanna said in the softest of voices. "I want you to know that in case you have any idea of running your cattle through the Keyhole tomorrow."

Herrod was silent for a long moment, tasting the bitter realization that he had been outmaneuvered by this frail girl from a Conconully gambling-den.

"I've got three-thousand-odd critters out on the flats," he said finally. "This fence won't stop them when they get started up Glacier Creek."

The sheriff sauntered over to the wire gate, leaning his elbows against the taut wire, his voice casual.

"Miss Laranjo owns the Keyhole, Herrod. I'll be camped on the rimrock with a shotgun and four or five deputies all this week. I'll g'arantee that not one hoof trespasses on this woman's property without her consent."

Herrod purpled, turning his gimlet stare on Del Troy, a brief wonderment touching him as he saw the livid bruises and scabbed cuts which had converted the Texan's face into a green-mottled caricature.

"This your idea, Troy? Blocking off the Canyon with a female's skirts?"

Troy appeared engrossed in shaking tobacco into a cigarette paper troughed between his fingers. Twisting the smoke and cementing it with a swipe of his tongue, the cowman directed his answer toward Shasta Ives.

"You've got gall, Herrod, talking about using a woman's skirts."

The inference in his voice stung Shasta, brought an amused smile to Roxanna's lips. Draping a Mexican shawl about her shoulders, the Spanish girl turned and headed toward her half-finished cabin. Gaddy and Troy remained in their tracks, watching Herrod's forming reactions with languid amusement.

"You got a legal right to haze those cattle as far as this fence," the sheriff averred, "seeing as how Miss Ives here has bought Whitey Crade's land. But that's as far as you'll go."

Doc Godette stirred in saddle, returning his whisky bottle to the military surgeon's kitbag strapped to his pommel. He eyed Herrod slantwise and drawled sagely, "Looks like you're out-foxed here, Bix. The law's closed this gate on us. You can't graze three thousand mossyhorns on Crade's homestead indefinitely."

Herrod picked up his reins, lashing his foreman with an angry glance. "Keep your horns out of this, Doc. Shasta, ride back to camp. I've got a few words for the tin star here that don't concern a woman."

Shasta Ives thrust out her chin, shaking her head adamantly. "No, Bix. Some of those cattle belong to Dollar. Whatever you're going to tell Mr. Gaddy, I have a right to hear."

The Conconully lawman laughed softly. "Nothing Herrod's got to say interests me, ma'am. He's caught pulling a sandy and he knows it. The devil himself couldn't force Roxie's fence as long as I've got a ca'tridge left or a crook in my trigger finger."

Herrod's face was apoplectic, but in Shasta's presence he forced himself to back down, yielding to the inevitable.

"You've closed off the front end of Flaming Canyon." He directed his venomous admission to Del Troy. "But there's still the back door, my Texan friend."

Herrod wheeled his blue roan and hammered off

78

across Crade's prairie, Doc Godette and the Dollar mistress riding after him.

"Back door," Del Troy echoed, firing his cigarette and turning his smoky eyes on the sheriff. "I don't savvy that lingo."

Sheriff Gaddy jabbed his corncob pipe between toothless gums and fished in his vest for a match.

"Easy to figger, son. Four-fifths of Flaming Canyon lies in the Twenty-Mile Strip. Herrod knows he's buffaloed at this end of the Canyon. He'll chouse his steers onto Okanogan Jones's range, make a deal with Jones, and before you know it you'll find Lazy H and Dollar beef spread over the back end of Flaming Canyon from hell to breakfast."

Troy thought that over at length, chewing on the possibilities that Gaddy was on the right track.

"Jones may be a greedy squaw man squatting on range he got from allotments to his Injun wife," Troy admitted, "but he's dead honest and square as a section corner. He leased Flaming Canyon to me. He won't turn around and open it to Herrod, not for all the gold Lazy H could fork over."

Roxanna joined them in time to hear Gaddy's reply: "Sure Okanogan Jones is honest. But he'll grant grazing rights to Herrod. You'd have to hire an army of line riders to keep Lazy H steers from drifting where the grass grows greenest, Troy. Which would be Flaming Canyon. The back door to your spread is wide open from the north."

Troy ground his fists together for a moment, then pushed by Roxanna Laranjo and disappeared behind the unfinished cabin. He reappeared a moment later astride his steeldust saddler.

"Take Roxie back to town, will you?" he asked

Gaddy. "You've spiked Herrod's guns. He won't cut this fence."

"What are you going to do, Del?" Roxanna asked anxiously, her eye on the six-gun thonged to Troy's leg.

"I'm riding up to Jones's place at Osoyoos Lake tonight. I've got to beat Herrod to the punch. This time tomorrow that trail herd will be scattering over the Strip. I've got to make sure Okanogan Jones will protect my lease."

Gaddy unfastened the wire gate and let Troy ride through. Roxanna's face was furrowed with worried lines as they stood watching Troy's departure, a tall and indomitable figure in the saddle, heading through the violet haze of sundown on his way out of Flaming Canyon.

"There goes a man, Roxie," the sheriff muttered through his pipe smoke, "who don't know when he's licked."

Roxanna's hand went in habitual gesture to the gold cross depended from her necklace. "If you think Del is licked, you don't know him as I do. He won't stop fighting Señor Herrod until he's dead."

Gaddy made a despondent gesture with his pipestem. "We did what we could for him, Roxie, but it wasn't enough. We just give Troy a breathin' spell that won't last out tomorrow. Once Herrod's beef hits Jones's Strip, the deal is out of my hands. My jurisdiction don't extend over the county line into the back half of Flaming Canyon. And Herrod knows that."

CHAPTER ELEVEN

BLOOD MONEY

THE TRAIL-WEARIED LAZY H CREW WAS TOSSING ITS supper dishes into the wreck pan of the chuck wagon when Herrod and Shasta Ives and Doc Godette cantered out of the sunset from Flaming Canyon.

They were hunkered over the tongue of the hoodlum wagon, eating the meal which the Dollar cook had rustled up for them, when they saw Del Troy leave the Canyon mouth and skirt the bedground on horseback, a mile distant and headed north.

Bix Herrod suppressed a half-formed impulse to order one of his crew to track the Texan down and make certain that Troy had taken his last ride. But Shasta's nearness precluded any such open violence. Herrod was aware that his fiancée was still nursing doubts as to the true cause of Fred Bolte's killing, and he was a man of great caution when the chips were down in a high-stake game.

"I wonder, now, where Troy would be riding?" Doc Godette, thinking out loud, voiced the same question which nagged the edge of Herrod's thoughts. "Let's see. There's Oro town and the Custom House at the Canadian line. Or Okanogan Jones's ranch at the head of Osoyoos Lake."

Herrod carried his tinware over to the chuck wagon and lighted a cigar. When he rejoined Shasta and the old medico, his plans had been shaped.

"Shasta, I hate to ask this favor of a woman. But I can't spare a man. Besides, you're the ideal person for the job."

81

"What job, Bix?"

Herrod squatted at the girl's side, his eyes fixed on the black-limned horizon to northward.

"It's a cinch Troy is heading for Jones's Ranch to try and talk the old squaw man into refusing to open the Strip to our beef, Shasta. And he might succeed. Jones is jealous of his power. He wouldn't like to see a big-scale rancher get a toehold in the Okanogan."

Shasta's eyes searched Herrod's face with grave concern. "What do you want me to do, Bix?"

"If you was to make a deal with Jones for your Dollar stuff, he wouldn't refuse. I know Jones, his vanities and his weaknesses. He's a sucker for a pretty face. Jones needn't know that Lazy H beef is mixed up with Dollar."

Doc Godette took his cue and ambled off toward the rope cavvy corral. When he returned, five minutes later, he led a leggy bay stallion with a Dollar brand on its rump.

Herrod had evidently given Shasta her instructions. As he helped her mount, he said apologetically, "You'll be perfectly safe, darling. It's only twenty miles to Osoyoos Lake and Jones's squaw will put you up overnight." He pushed a weighted leather poke into her saddlebag. "Money talks with Jones. Remember to keep Lazy H out of this. Dicker with Jones for grazing rights for three thousand-odd head."

Belatedly Shasta bent down for his parting kiss, feeling as always an unaccountable reluctance to share his caress. "Summer graze will be waiting for us when the herd crosses the Strip tomorrow, Bix," she promised him.

"Your charms worked with Crade," Doc Godette put in slyly. "An old gaffer like Okanogan Jones will be a pushover."

The darkness hid Shasta's abashed grimace.

"I'm not proud of my conquest over Crade, Doc. What good does his homestead do us now? We're out a thousand dollars, that's all."

With that she was gone, spurring off toward the north, soon lost in the roundabout shadows. Herrod turned to Godette and grufled irritably, "Dammit, why did you have to mention Crade? A man's got to play his hand the way it's dealt him."

Godette shuffled off to get his bedroll from the hoodlum wagon.

Herrod finished his cigar, lost in his thoughts. In spite of the impasse which Roxanna Laranjo had flung in his path today, the Lazy H man was in smug spirits. Flaming Canyon was far from lost to him. Its use was vital to his summer plans, for he was short-handed and once his beef was thrown onto Flaming Canyon grass, keeping them bunched until the fall round-up would be a simple thing to accomplish with a skeleton crew.

The Conconully sheriff was nullified as an opposing factor, once the Yakima pool herd was north of the county line. Gaddy had already been dismissed from Herrod's mind. Toward Roxanna, Herrod owned a steady and mounting hatred—it galled his masculine vanity to have been outwitted by a female, and he realized he'd have to take care of her sooner or later.

With Shasta absent on her overnight trek to Jones's Ranch, Herrod decided to sleep at Crade's shack instead of with his crew. He went over to where his crew was playing poker on spread-out blankets by lantern light and ordered his horse brought up, and then returned to the chuck wagon to finish his smoke.

He was waiting there when a rider took shape against the star-powdered skyline and, after hailing the cook over by the smoldering campfire, dismounted and engaged the pot-wrangler in an animated conversation.

Mentally dismissing the newcomer as a grubliner cadging a meal, Herrod was vaguely surprised when the rider called him by name, only arm's length away.

"Don't you know me, Herrod? I'm Whitey Crade."

Herrod straightened, staring at the disheveled wreck of a man who stood limned in the guttering pulse of the campfire's light. "Good lord, man, what happened to you? You look like you come off second best in a tussle with a buzz saw."

Crade dropped his eyes, turned to put his face in shadow. His clothing was in rags, his nose was a swollen monstrosity against his battered fish-belly white face, and both eyes were puffed to misshapen slits.

"Tangled with Troy over at Conconully yesterday. The sheriff give me my walkin'-papers. That's why I'm here."

Herrod pursed his lips thoughtfully, remembering the marks of combat he had noted on Troy's features over at the Keyhole earlier this evening.

"Troy sore because you double-crossed him, eh?"

Crade spat through a wide gap in his teeth where Troy's fists had caved in his jaw. "To hell with Troy. I'll kill the sonofabitch one of these days. Herrod, I want to rent my lass'-rope to Lazy H for the summer. Hear you're shorthanded. I'm a top hand."

It was on the tip of Herrod's tongue to refuse Crade. He knew the albino's mercuric temperament, his unstable ways. Loyalty and industry were not in Whitey Crade. He was a trouble-maker on any crew, a bunkhouse agitator to be avoided like a plague, no matter how shorthanded an outfit might be.

But the curt refusal died without utterance. A new

84

possibility of Crade's usefulness to Lazy H dawned in Herrod's brain.

"You say you aim to settle your score with Del Troy. You can do that and draw Lazy H pay to boot, Crade."

The albino spat again, rubbing his hands together. Before he could answer, the night wrangler came up with Herrod's saddle horse. Waiting until the wrangler had withdrawn out of earshot, Herrod played his ace.

"Troy's riding up the Strip to Jones's Ranch tonight, Whitey. He'll probably be back sometime tomorrow. You any idea what trail he'd take?"

Whitey Crade's face took on a malevolent vitality.

"Sure He'd cut over from Osoyoos Lake to Oro and the Wannacut, hit the Loomis Road at Lily Basin, and follow it back to Flaming Canyon. I've made the ride with him a dozen times."

Herrod handed his reins to the albino and put a hand on Crade's shoulder. "Here's your horse. You'll find a couple of quarts of smooth bourbon in the alforja pockets. I can't use your rope, Crade. But I'll rent your guns."

Crade stepped into saddle, fumbling with the straps of the saddle pouch to check on the two bottles of whisky there.

"How you handle Troy is up to you," Herrod went on. "I want him out of the way. So do you."

Avarice kindled in the albino's swollen, puffy eyes. "What's in it for me besides the fun of seeing Troy drop and kick, Herrod? A man can't wet his stomach on revenge."

The night masked Herrod's contempt. "Shasta gave you a thousand dollars of my money to sell out Troy. I'll double that if you bring me proof that Troy's dead."

Crade leaned from stirrups to shake on the deal.

"I'll fetch you Troy's topknot, if you say so," he grinned, and rode off into the night, guided by the far cold gleam of Polaris.

CHAPTER TWELVE

HERROD'S ACE OF TRUMPS

THE CLANG OF AN IRON TRIANGLE ROUSED DEL TROY at daybreak. He had arrived at Okanogan Jones's place too late to dicker with the squaw man, and had spent the night in the long barked-log bunkhouse which Jones rented to Cariboo Trail travelers at five dollars per head, including breakfast.

The self-styled king of the Twenty-Mile Strip had built himself a rustic citadel here at the south end of Osoyoos Lake, and he did a thriving trade. The mess hall adjoining the bunkhouse was jammed with boisterous patrons this morning, a motley cross section of frontier humanity which had never failed to intrigue Troy on his past visits to Jones's headquarters.

He shared the washroom with bearded Canuck trappers from Hudson's Bay; cheechakos from Europe and the East who, despairing of booking passage on Alaska-bound steamers, were attempting the overland route to the Klondike gold fields; buckskin-clad woodsmen; frock-coated gamblers seeking refuge from the law; stolid-faced cavalrymen from the army post at Fort Colville, assigned to border patrol duty; lumberjacks and miners; and shifty-eyed men with the look of the owlhoot on them—they were met here at Okanogan Jones's crossroads blockhouse.

The squaw man's chair at the head of the mess table

was vacant when Troy entered the hall. But his portly Indian wife, Tenas Josie, was on hand to supervise her corps of giggling half-breed daughters who plied to and from the kitchen with endless platters heaped with venison, moose steaks, steaming mugs of black coffee, wheat cakes and jellies. and country butter in ten-pound lumps.

A hairy-faced prospector en route to the States from the Yukon was dominating the table conversation when Troy found himself a place at the crowded benches. The Alaska miner wore three chains of yellow nuggets looped ostentatiously across his unbuttoned plucked-beaver coat, and he was boasting of a carpetbag full of gold dust which he had deposited in Okanogan Jones's safe for the night.

"Ye're all damned fools not to pull stakes and head for Dawson, friends!" the miner spoke through a mouth crammed with venison. "In six days with a Long Tom an' a dishpan I grubbed twenty thousand dollars out of Bonanza Creek. Plenty more where that come from, free for the takin'. Me, I'm headin' for Seattle to paint the burg red before I head back north for another fling."

There was a momentary lull in the babble of talk, and Okanogan Jones made his dramatic entry into the mess hall. He was a wizened little man in his middle sixties, dressed in fringed buckskin and parfleche leggings, with a Mormon's black hat topping his leonine mane of hair and a shock of cinnamon whiskers bracketing his pippin red cheeks.

This husband of the Moses squaw, Tenas Josie, had hewn his niche in Washington politics and was now at the heyday of his power. It had been Okanogan Jones who had made a personal trek to Washington and influenced Congress to set aside the Twenty-Mile Strip from the Indian lands which were closed to white settlement.

Jones was the undisputed monarch of thousands of sections of Cascade timberland and its unplumbed mineral wealth. Osoyoos Lake was a Jones cistern. He had built his blockhouse here in the days of Indian warfare and when his scalp loomed as a tempting trophy for Chief Moses's tomahawk-wielding braves, he scotched that threat by marrying Tenas Josie and adding her allotments to his kingdom.

But Del Troy's eyes were not on Okanogan Jones as the leather-caparisoned autocrat of the frontier made his entrance. On Jones's arm, like a queen entering her royal palace, was Shasta Ives. She took the extra chair which Tenas Josie had placed alongside her husband's split-cedar throne at the head of the table, her eyes flashing with excitement as she saw the impact her arrival had made on this uncombed, unkempt assemblage.

Some half-forgotten sense of gallantry touched the mob as it wolfed down its food, and to a man they got to their feet, waiting as Okanogan Jones adjusted the chair behind his guest.

"Be seated, gents!" Jones invited, obviously pleased by this tribute from his rough patrons. "My guest of honor, boys—Miss Shasta Ives. Owns the Dollar ranch down Yakima way."

Del Troy's eyes met Shasta's and he knew that his trip had been in vain. Okanogan Jones was eating out of the girl's hand; he had opened the Strip to Dollar and Lazy H beef. He knew that with a despairing intuition that brooked no hope to the contrary.

Like Crade, like Jones, he thought bitterly, and his voracious appetite deserted him. Herrod played his cards for what they were worth. And Shasta was his ace of trumps.

"A cowgirl, eh?" spoke up the loquacious Klondiker. "Ma'am, you're overlookin' a bonanza in yore own back yard. Up in Juneau an' Ketchikan this minute, beefsteaks as thin as a bootsole are fetchin' an ounce of dust, an' no fresh meat to be had."

Okanogan Jones speared himself a hunk of roast moose and signaled one of his daughters for the coffee pot. "So?" chuckled the oldster. "Nineteen dollars for a tough beefsteak. Miss Shasta, maybe you ought to move your herd on across the border to Alasky. Them mossyhorns would be worth their weight in gold up yander."

Del Troy, watching Shasta in spite of himself, saw that the blowhard from the Klondike had her undivided attention.

"Is that feasible, sir?" she asked the miner. "I mean, can cattle be driven overland to the gold camps?"

The Klondiker, flattered, wiped his beard with a greasy palm and leaned across the table toward Shasta.

"Why not? Once out of the Cariboo country, you got the Telegraph Trail straight across Yukon Territory. What do you sell a cow for here in Washington?"

Shasta's glance raked down the table to fix on Del Troy. "Well, I—that is, we expect to net twenty dollars a head at Seattle this fall."

The Bonanza Creeker scoffed. "Hell's fire, ma'am—beggin' your pardon—at Dawson that same cow would fetch five hundred bucks. You got all summer to drive your beef north. You got an army of beef-hongry miners waitin' for a market, an' thousands arrivin' up the trail every week. I tell you, you could make yourself a million."

Okanogan Jones waggled his head dissentingly.

"He's joshin', Miss Shasta. Don't believe half o' the hogwash you hear at my table. Why, you got better'n fifteen hundred mile o' mountain an' forest betwixt here an' the Klondike. A bighorn goat couldn't foller this Telegraph Trail our friend speaks of. You let your beef fatten up on the Strip this summer an' don't go fillin' your perty little head with crazy notions."

Troy left the dining-hall while the petty argument raged between Okanogan Jones and the Klondike optimist. He smoked through a dozen cigarettes before Jones and Shasta Ives left the mess hall and headed for the horse barn.

One of Tenas Josie's daughters was holding a stirrup for Shasta when Troy entered the barn. Mounting, Shasta said to Troy without preliminaries, "Bix tells me that Fred Bolte was knifed to death in Wenatchee on the way north, Del."

"Did he? Then I'm a liar "

She flushed under the whiplash of his words.

"I am aware that you hate my future husband," she said candidly. "I regret that more than I can tell you. But it occurred to me you might have been mistaken in the identity of the ambusher you shot over at Grand Coulee that night."

Troy laughed softly. "You might ask Doc Godette about the Stetson with the fishhooks in the band that I gave Bix at Brewster ferry," he said. "No. Forget I said that. Godette knows who butters his biscuits. He wouldn't double-cross Bix."

She stared at him numbly, her eyes unaccountably moist. Then she wheeled her bay stallion and, with a choked word of thanks to Okanogan Jones and the half-Indian girl, she sent her saddler on a dead run toward the Cariboo Trail.

Troy turned to Okanogan Jones, surprising his intent stare.

"Don't say it, Troy!" the squaw man snapped testily. "I already know why you're here. You had your ride for nothin'. Miss Ives told me you aimed to bulldoze me into closin' the Strip to her beef. You ought to be ashamed of yourself."

Troy leaned the point of his shoulder against the barn door. "Mind telling me about the deal you closed with Shasta?"

Jones scowled, and then, because he liked this hard-bitten Texan, relented from his first impulse. "She'll pay a dollar a head for summer graze, subject to my tally at the round-up this fall."

Troy tugged his lower lip. "Shasta owns around six hundred head of cattle. You don't stand to make your taxes, Jones."

Okanogan Jones bent a queer stare at the cowman. "You're mistaken She told me she'd be grazing around three thousand head this summer. The herd hits the Strip today."

"Sure it does," Troy said, and drove across the clincher he had been leading up to. "The bulk of it Lazy H beef, belonging to Bix Herrod. Bix used the girl to run a sandy on both of us, Jones. Lazy H has its eye on Flaming Canyon, not your rough land. That's why I rode up here to see you last night."

Okanogan Jones was a fair and judicious man. For the first time he sensed the fact that all was not right, that he had been duped into putting his signature to an agreement without inquiring into its possible ramifications.

"The hell you say, Troy!" he blurted. "The girl didn't

91

specify what brands those cattle carried. I naturally assumed it was old Colonel Sam's Dollar." He grinned bleakly. "No fool like an old one. I've been took by a perty smile. My lease didn't specify Dollar or any other brand."

Troy had Jones on the defensive now and he pushed his advantage. "Jones, you leased Flaming Canyon to me. If I furnish the wire and posts, can I count on your crews fencing off the coulees running into my lease, to keep Lazy H and Dollar cattle off my grass this summer?"

Jones fidgeted uncomfortably. "I ain't got the men to spare for a fencin' job, son. Keepin' Flamin' Canyon clear of drifters will be up to you, not me."

Troy had his answer, knew he had played his cards and lost. Technically, Flaming Canyon was out of bounds to Lazy H and Dollar beef. Actually, the contract Jones had consummated with Shasta Ives this very morning was an open invitation to let Herrod's beef roam where it willed.

"I don't like the idea of Herrod movin' in on me any better'n you do, son," Okanogan Jones went on. "The man's ambitious to ramrod Washington State, I can see that. But it looks to me as if he's got us backed into a corner. Say the word, and I'll refund the money you paid me for that lease."

Troy shook his head, walking over to a stall where his steeldust mustang was hitched.

"No. Looks like this is up to me and Herrod to fight out, Jones. I was a fool for thinking you could help me."

While Troy saddled and bridled, Jones paced in the background, tugging his red whiskers nervously.

"Beats me how a four-fiusher like this Herrod roped hisself a thoroughbred like this Shasta woman," he grumbled. "You reckon that Shasta filly come up here an' made a fool out o' me, son?"

Troy ducked low under the door lintel as he spurred out of the barn.

"You figger it out," he retorted. "*Hasta luego.*"

CHAPTER THIRTEEN

BULL' S-EYE FOR A BUSHWHACKER

SHASTA IVES LET HER LEGGY BAY WORK OFF ITS morning steam until the green peach orchards marking the limit of Okanogan Jones's domain were a mile behind her. Then she settled the stallion into a long lope and turned her thoughts inward.

The heiress to Dollar ranch had spent most of her twenty years in saddle; she rode with the supple ease of a centaur and a horseback jaunt of a crisp morning was invariably conducive to mental excursions which left her oblivious to passing scenes.

Thinking and self-communion were yokes the girl would have gladly shed in favor of enjoying the new landscape this morning, but there were things crowding her consciousness now which were not to be ignored.

The fact of Fred Bolte's violent death had left her untouched emotionally, for she had always held her fiancé's bodyguard in stern disfavor. The hang of Bolte's tied-down guns, on a frontier where riders ordinarily avoided the added weight of armament except on dress-up occasions, stamped Bolte in Shasta's eyes as a man whose presence on the Lazy H payroll was due to his trigger skill rather than his worth as a range hand.

But she had been careful never to question the

reasons why her handsome, swashbuckling suitor had filled his Lazy H bunkhouse with casehardened men like Bolte and Doc Godette. When her ailing father had hinted that Bix Herrod hired men as Colonel Sam had once picked soldiers for a sortie behind the Yankee lines, for their shooting skill alone, she had charitably suggested that Herrod, unlike her father, preferred to have Texans working for him.

Whereas Shasta had her private doubts concerning most of the Lazy H roster, she was under no illusions about Doc Godette's morals. His lecherous eye never touched her without making her feel somehow unclean. She saw in him the disease-ravaged shell of a man. But Doc Godette had ministered to her father during Colonel Sam's final illness last winter, and on that score alone she tolerated Godette's lascivious innuendoes and forgave him his uncouth ways.

Even after Colonel Sam's death and her decision to wear Herrod's ring, Shasta had turned a deaf ear to whispers which came her way. This morning she was remembering a conversation she had overheard in the Dollar blacksmith shop when the Colonel's men gathered there to roundside while horseshoes cooled in the vat. They had branded Herrod for an outright rustler and worse. But loyalty to a future husband came first with Shasta, and she had dismissed the talk as bunkhouse gossip, without foundation.

But now Fred Bolte was dead, and a lone homesteader from Flaming Canyon had openly admitted killing Bolte in self-defense. She had Herrod's assurance that the wrangler had died in a drunken brawl with a Wenatchee harlot. Which version was the true one?

She realized that Del Troy was Herrod's enemy, and

therefore her enemy. A drifter without so much as a cow to slap his own iron on, Troy was harvesting the lush hay crop in Flaming Canyon to the detriment of her cattle as well as Herrod's.

The fact that Del Troy had the power to stir unguessed wellsprings in the core of her, by the briefest of glances or the inflection of his voice when he spoke to her, had come to assume the proportions of something shameful and clandestine in Shasta's secret appraisal of herself.

Listening to Herrod's arguments concerning Troy, Shasta had been convinced of her own free will that ruthless methods were in order. She had stood by, tacitly condoning Herrod's leasing of the Brewster ferry which cut Troy off from his freight traffic east of the Columbia. Guilt had touched her only obliquely when she had connived with Whitey Crade to betray Troy.

And in arranging a summer lease with Okanogan Jones this morning, she now realized that her business proposition had been predicated on half-truths which the squaw man had accepted in good faith. Bix Herrod was probably right in believing that Jones would not allow Lazy H beef to enter the Strip.

Last night, with Herrod's magical personality throwing its spell over her, the means justified the ends so far as Jones was concerned. But now, with the first flush of her easy conquest behind her, Shasta Ives found herself wondering what the ghost of her father might be thinking of the chicanery she had employed in opening the Strip to Lazy H cattle.

She had done nothing wrong in a legal sense of the word. She was reasonably clear of conscience on that point. But in thwarting Del Troy and in deceiving Okanogan Jones as to her true purpose for closing a deal

95

for summer graze, she had strayed sadly afield from the teachings of her intrepid old sire.

Her self-condemnation made a vicious circle, beginning and ending with the mysterious death of Fred Bolte. She was unwilling to let her thoughts touch on the possibility that the man whose children she intended to bear, whose name she would shortly assume, was a man capable of sending one of his men on an ambush mission.

Yet Del Troy's candor reminded her uncomfortably of her father's mannerisms. Either Troy or Herrod had lied about the true facts of Fred Bolte's death. And Troy did not strike her as a man who would boast about a murder he had not committed.

These things were festering in Shasta's brain when disaster struck her on a stony patch of the Cariboo Trail. Her bay saddler, hitting a reckless lope along the road, without warning plunged a forehoof into a weed-shrouded gopher hole and went down in full stride.

Inbred experience saved the girl serious injury as she instinctively kicked free of oxbow stirrups and, using the saddlehorn for a springboard, vaulted over the bay's head as it hit the dirt and slewed around on the pivot of its trapped hoof, the snap of bone sounding clear as a breaking stick in her ears.

The animal's first agonized scream was timed with her landing on all fours on the flinty earth. Even as she came to her feet, shrouded with drifting dust and shocked to the roots of her teeth, she realized the bay must be put out of its misery.

Colonel Sam Ives had always insisted that his daughter carry a Smith and Wesson in her saddle pocket to use against a rattlesnake or range coyote, or for emergencies such as this one.

She had owned the bay since it was foaled. It had been a gift from her father. Moving in a stupor of grief, she unbuckled the saddlebag and took out the revolver. The bay's anguished eyes wrenched her as she put the .32 muzzle behind the animal's ear, looked away, and pulled the trigger.

She could not bring herself to remain beside the dead bay. Instead she moved off the trail and seated herself on a rocky shelf which jutted out into the sliding green waters of the Okanogan, there to give way to a storm of girlish sobs.

Her grief was not yet spent when a rataplan of hoofbeats reached her ears. Turning, she stared through flooding tears to see the whip-lean figure of Del Troy reining his steelduster alongside the slain stallion on the road.

"Toughest thing that can happen to a rider, ma'am," he said gently, removing his Stetson. "Horses are people to me, same as to you. But you did the only merciful thing."

He had dismounted by the time she had climbed the slope and was loosening the bay's latigo. She watched, wiping her eyes with her neck scarf, as he extricated her saddle from the dead weight of the carcass. He stripped his Brazos hull from the steelduster and replaced it with her own gear.

"Alamo's gentle," he said, swapping bridles. "I can pick him up from the Lazy H cavvy later."

She sank to her knees beside the dead bay, stroking its glossy mane as a bereaved mother might caress a child. "But I can't leave you on foot, Del. You can't cover the twenty miles back to Flaming Canyon in those star boots."

He hoisted his saddle over a shoulder, deriving a

strange thrill from her use of his first name.

"I won't have to. Jones will lend me a bronc."

He offered his hand and she mounted the steeldust mustang, gathering up the reins. Tears were close to her lashes as she regarded her dead bay.

Reading her thought, Troy said, "I'll have Jones send down a man to bury your pet, Shasta. Next time you ride up this way you can fix up a headboard to suit your fancy. I won't let the coyotes molest anything."

For a long moment their eyes met and held, and again Shasta felt the stormy rebellion in her heart, the half-sensed twinge of disloyalty toward the man she was engaged to marry.

"I'm sorry we're on opposite sides, you and I," she said simply. "I wish we could be friends."

He took her hand on that, but the spell was broken and a brittle note entered his voice as he recalled her mission to Osoyoos Lake and the disaster it meant for him. "As long as Herrod keeps his steers off Flaming Canyon graze, there'll be no trouble," he said bluntly. *"Hasta la vista."*

He could not know that his parting Spanish idiom, a throwback to his Texas years, had been the identical last words her father had uttered. He mistook the sudden sobs which choked her as a woman's grief for a favorite pony. When she had gotten a grip on herself, Del Troy was already a hundred yards away, trudging back toward Okanogan Jones's ranch with his saddle and bridle.

She turned south once more after a whispered farewell to her dead horse, and followed the Cariboo Trail through a break in the foothill timber to enter a broad mountain meadow dappled with wild lilies in full bloom and bordered with rhododendron jungles limb-heavy with flowering masses.

This was Lily Basin, though she was new to this country and did not know it. She sent Troy's steelduster into an easy singlefoot jog.

Whitey Crade had spent the long night among the pines that crowned a hogback overlooking the Lily Basin road. Sleep had been denied him, for the throb of bruised muscles and splintered ribs was not to be eased by anything except the passage of time. His toxic personality had been further unbalanced by the virulence of the hatred which seethed in his warped brain, a hatred which had had its beginning in the brawl with Del Troy at the Loop-Loop deadfall and his banishment from Conconully.

The bourbon bottles which Bix Herrod had sent with him from the Lazy H cow camp last night were empty now, tossed aside in the knee-high Russian thistles which concealed Crade's presence overlooking Lily Basin.

The hogback's crest gave him a view of the entire length of the Cariboo Trail where it crossed the meadow; and he knew that it was a matter of time before Del Troy would come within range of his Winchester; homeward bound from Jones's Ranch.

Whisky and brooding hate and the frustrations which had become a part of the albino's basic character had fused to make Whitey Crade irrational, edgy as a coiled rattler in dogdays. His rabbit-pink eyes had studied the road below ever since dawn's early light had filtered into the basin below his ambuscade.

The liquor in his veins had put Whitey Crade's vision out of focus, made his head reel. But he was not too drunk or cold or hungry to miss the rider on the steeldust mustang who came in sight through the timbered gateway now.

The tension mounted in Crade as he reached for the .30-30 carbine at his side and checked the shell in its breech. He thrust the octagonal barrel over a lava chunk and lined the sights tentatively on a flat patch of road directly opposite his hiding-place, in the path of the oncoming rider.

To Whitey Crade, waiting with the impatience of a spider in its lair, the identity of that rider was beyond question. His eyes, never keen because of their abnormal pigmentation, did not have the power to focus on details. But the erect posture of the horsebacker told him it was Del Troy; so did the sweep of the Texas sombrero.

If he needed final and decisive proof that his long-awaited target was now within gun range, the steeldust mustang supplied that proof. Crade had been with Troy when the horse, then a yearling, had fallen into their mustang trap in the Guadalupes out of El Paso one winter five years back. Troy had selected Alamo for his own personal mount on the long-gone fuzztail hunt.

The rifle barrel wavered slightly as Crade notched his sights on the rider's chest, following the loping steelduster in a level arc. He pulled a deep breath into his lungs to steady his aim, cuddling the walnut stock against a bruised cheek. When the steelduster was directly opposite his ambush, Whitey Crade squeezed off his shot.

The butt plate recoiled against his shoulder and Whitey Crade reared to his knees, fanning the smudge of gunsmoke away with his hat.

As through a windowpane swimming with the beat of raindrops, Crade saw the steelduster galloping empty-saddled across the meadow, its rider a shapeless, motionless sprawl on the road below.

Bix Herrod had promised two thousand dollars cash on the barrelhead for proof of Del Troy's death. His guns, his hat—any symbol to back up Crade's report.

But shame and panic seized the albino now, shocking him cold sober. He flung his carbine aside in the weeds as if it had been a scaly reptile. Del Troy lay dead on the Cariboo Trail. But consummated revenge left a flat, acid taste in Crade's mouth.

He slogged back over the hillcrest to where he had left Bix Herrod's mount. Tardily the realization came to Whitey Crade that his bullet had snuffed the life from the only man who had ever befriended him in his misspent career.

That damning knowledge would haunt Whitey Crade to his grave.

CHAPTER FOURTEEN

A TERRIBLE MISTAKE

THE SMUDGE OF BIX HERROD'S NORTHERING CATTLE herd once more lay in a ragged pillowing mass against the southern skyline when Del Troy left Okanogan Jones's ranch astride an appaloosa mare the squaw man had loaned him.

His unscheduled return to the Osoyoos Lake blockhouse had paid off with an unexpected windfall of business. Jones, making a subtle peace offering to mollify Troy after his refusal to defend the Texan's grazing rights in Flaming Canyon, had come forth with the news that he had purchased a sawmill in the upper Methow Valley. Jones had a yen to go into the logging business for himself, to tap the rich source of revenue which had hitherto been Steen Slankard's monopoly.

Thus, when Troy set out for Flaming Canyon at midmorning, he carried with him a lucrative contract for a month's work of dismantling and freighting the mill, complete with donkey engine, across the mountains to the site which Jones's timber cruisers would select for future logging operations.

Troy knew that Jones had the wagons and the manpower to do his own freighting, but he saw no reason to decline this largess and he insisted on a written agreement. This prospect of adding substantially to his cash reserve meant the difference, for Troy, of starting his beef herd in the fall or postponing it for an indefinite period of time.

But the advent of the Lazy H and Dollar pool herd, written in the trail of dust which feathered the skyline ahead of him, robbed Troy of the full savor of his improved outlook.

He knew he would be powerless to prevent Herrod's beef from encroaching on the rich grama grass which stood high in Flaming Canyon this season. Appealing to the federal courts for an injunction requiring Lazy H to police its own lease was out of the question; by the time the ponderous legal machinery got in motion, the damage would be done. And fencing off the canyon's innumerable entering coulees would take months to accomplish.

A depression that was unusual for the man settled on Troy as he put his borrowed mare down the trail. He turned his thoughts toward Shasta Ives, wondering how a woman could look at a man with the wide-eyed sincerity of a nun, and yet be capable of baiting a trap for a shrewd man like Okanogan Jones; a woman who could break her heart over the loss of a pet animal, and

102

yet cheapen herself into beguiling a weakling like Whitey Crade into selling a partner down the river for a few pieces of Judas gold.

Thought of Crade brought a sadness to Troy, rather than any remembered anger. He wondered where Crade was this morning—probably headed for Texas. Knowing Crade's inferior mentality, his childish dependence on guidance from others, Troy doubted if the albino would reach the Rio Grande. Born under an evil star, damned by his physical handicap, Crade was an object for pity, not hate. He would probably wind up in a cowtown alley with a knife in his ribs, or spill his blood across some line-camp poker table en route to his native Panhandle.

Troy's mind was occupied with these dour prophecies as he gigged the appaloosa through the timbered mouth of Lily Basin. The mare whinnied at sight of an empty-saddled horse grazing on the meadow floor a hundred yards off the trail. Troy's following glance identified the foraging horse as his own steelduster.

His first thought was that Alamo had thrown Shasta Ives, though he had seen enough of her riding ability to doubt that such an accident could have happened. The next instant, his swiveling gaze searched out the sprawled figure of the girl, lying in the wagon road ahead.

He roweled the appaloosa to a gallop, cold dread knotting his throat muscles as he skidded to a halt alongside the girl, saw the clotted blood which had soaked the wheat-blond tresses on the nape of her neck.

Forgetting that he was on a borrowed mount, he vaulted from saddle and ground-hitched the mare, only to see her snort at realization of her freedom and gallop off into the meadow.

Down on one knee beside Shasta, Troy parted the

103

blood-soaked hair to reveal the shallow furrow cut through the flesh above the backbone, like a trace of crimson chalk.

Such a long, straight wound would not have been sustained by falling on a sharp rock.

Bullet crease. A bullet meant for me.

The rise and fall of the girl's lungs as he lifted her was Troy's first proof that the slug had not scored the spinal column, killing her instantly. He judged from the amount of blood she had lost from a relatively shallow wound that the gunshot he had heard on his way back to Okanogan Jones's ranch must have been the one which had knocked the girl from saddle.

Carrying his unconscious burden over to a cushion of dew-moist grass, he lowered her gently and loosened her shirt collar. Healthy color was already suffusing her face; her pulse was steady and strong. The stunned nerves at the base of her skull were rallying and she would, in all probability, come out of her coma suddenly and completely, unaware of any lapse of time.

A whistle brought his steelduster cantering over from the rhododendron brakes. By the time the horse reached the road, Shasta's eyes had fluttered open and she was attempting feebly to prop herself up on her elbows.

Incoherent syllables formed on her lips as Troy stepped over to his horse and unlooped his canvas waterbag from the horn. Using the girl's silken neck scarf for a swab, he cleansed the bullet nick as best he could, washed the dirt and gore from her hair, and bound the scarf about her neck to protect the exposed flesh from dust.

"Reckon you run into a dry-gulch trap that was set for me, ma'am," he told her, holding her head while she drank from the spout of the waterbag. "Somebody who knew my steelduster and was too far off to see who was riding it." She did not register what he had said, he knew; but she was able to sit up by herself. Her eyes were sightless, glazed orbs as she stared at him, her brain still groping through a black tunnel.

Scanning the surrounding meadow, Troy saw where an ambusher could have had innumerable choices of hideouts. For all he knew, the bushwhacker might be lurking within gunshot range at this moment; and the thought sent Troy back to his horse, snaking the Winchester out of its scabbard.

"We'll ride on together, Shasta, just in case," Troy grinned, jerking the lever of the .30-30. "You take it easy while I dab my twine on Jones's mare."

The appaloosa had not bolted far. Precluding any necessity for using his own horse, Troy unbuckled his sisal lariat from the pommel, shook out a loop, and, carrying his rifle, set off toward the grazing mare.

That was the first coherent picture of Del Troy which came to clear focus in Shasta Ives's bullet-numbed brain. The throbbing pain which scalded her neck nape brought her hand up to touch the bandage which Troy had put there; she saw the freshly coagulated blood which smeared her finger tips.

Through the mysterious powers of association which ruled her brain at the moment, Shasta connected the wound on her neck with the rifle which Del Troy was carrying as he headed toward the appaloosa. And to Shasta, the combination of evidence which her eyes beheld added up to one appalling conclusion—Del Troy had overtaken her on the trail and attempted to kill her.

With a choked scream, the girl pulled herself to her feet and, seizing the steelduster's saddle horn and cantle rim, dragged herself clumsily astride.

Terror whipped the girl's distraught senses as she clapped spurs to the mustang's flanks and sent it rocketing down the grassy basin, expecting any instant to hear the crack of Troy's rifle and to feel the stunning jolt of a bullet between her shoulder blades.

Her sudden getaway spooked the appaloosa mare, sending it off at a tangent before Troy could get within roping range of the fractious animal.

His own puzzlement and dismay at seeing the girl's sudden flight made him yell out, but his shout, instead of bringing reason to Shasta Ives, made the girl redouble her frantic spurring of the steelduster.

By the time Troy put his loop on the mare, Shasta was out of sight. An hour's headlong ride through the timbered foothills cleared her head in a physical sense, but her hysteria toward Del Troy remained, confusing and outraging her.

The dust of the Yakima trail herd was her guiding beacon as she hit the open flats at the south border of the Twenty-Mile Strip. Giving Troy's horse a chance to blow, Shasta heard the remote cacophony of bawling cattle as Herrod's herd topped the flat horizon ahead of her.

Troy had apparently made no attempt to overtake her. She had not glimpsed the Texan at any time during her wild flight.

She located the chuck wagon marking the crew's noon camp, and put the steelduster in that direction.

Bix Herrod and Doc Godette were eating their noon meal apart from the crew when they spotted the oncoming rider. Earlier this morning, Whitey Crade had galloped in from that identical direction, giving out a gibbering, half-intelligible version of Del Troy's ambush death up in Lily Basin.

"Looks like Shasta astraddle that mustang of Troy's,"

106

Doc Godette commented, squinting his cataract-rimmed eyes into the sun glare. "How could that be, you reckon? She wouldn't swap her favorite Skeeter hoss for that steelduster, even if she run across it after Crade bushwhacked Troy."

Herrod blew on his coffee to cool it, his own eyes narrowing with a grim premonition.

"She'll confirm Crade's story, most likely," the Lazy H boss grunted. "Keep your smart remarks to yourself, Doc."

The two men came to their feet as Shasta rode up and half-slid, half-fell out of saddle into Herrod's waiting arms.

"You're hurt!" Herrod exclaimed, seeing the dried blood on the neckerchief which girdled her throat. "Doc, break out your kitbag. Shasta's skinned up."

The girl clung to him, trembling.

"Del Troy—shot me," she panted hysterically. "Loaned me—his horse—after Skeeter broke his leg in a gopher hole. Then Troy—trailed me—and tried to bushwhack me, Bix."

Herrod pushed her out to arm's length, his eyes frogging with disbelief.

"How's that again? Pull yourself together, woman. You say Troy took a shot at you?"

She nodded vehemently. "I saw him walking back to the horse he borrowed from Okanogan Jones when I came to," she said. "He had his rifle in his hand. It couldn't have been a minute after he grazed me."

Shasta spoke with complete surety, unaware that she was distorting the truth, for the time-lapse following the impact of the slug which had snuffed out her senses had seemed scarcely longer than the space between clock-ticks.

"He shot me, Bix. I tell you, Troy shot at me."

Doc Godette came over from the campfire where he had put his surgical tools to boil in a tin can. He had overheard Shasta's hysterical narrative, and even as his eye met Herrod's over the girl's shoulder, he knew that the Lazy H boss had surmised the real truth.

Whitey Crade's vague, repetitious recital of having shot Del Troy and set the steeldust mustang astray in Lily Basin gave logic to what had really happened. Crade's ambush bullet had dropped Shasta from saddle, providentially with only a superficial wound. Switched riders had confused the drunken albino.

During her period of insensibility, Troy must have arrived on the scene. In all likelihood he had put the makeshift bandage on her neck before she regained consciousness.

"You heard what Shasta said, Doc!" Herrod clipped, his voice vibrating with quick triumph. "While you're patching up Shasta I'll round up three or four of the boys. We've got a job to do."

Shasta Ives, yielding herself to the skilled hands of the segundo who had never lost his surgeon's genius of yesteryear, took no interest in her surroundings until, five minutes later, Bix Herrod rode up, flanked by four Lazy H cowhands. Doc Godette's line-back grulla accompanied them, saddled and bridled. From the pommel of Herrod's saddle swung a coil of hemp rope.

"Where—where are you going?" Shasta's voice held a sudden panic at sight of the rope. "What are you going to do?"

Herrod's mouth was a grim seam as he slapped a palm on the coil of hemp he had picked up from the hoodlum wagon. "Ride up the trail to meet Troy. There's only one brand of medicine for a polecat who'd try to shoot a woman."

Shasta ran forward, forcing him to halt his horse or run her down.

"You can't lynch him, Bix. Turn him over to the sheriff, and I'll testify at his trial. But don't put Troy's ghost between us now."

Something in the girl's voice warned Herrod to go easy. "All right," he growled. "I'll hold Troy for the law, if that's how you want it. That's a promise."

Doc Godette climbed into saddle and the horse-backers galloped off in a surge of lifting dust.

"We got the deadwood on Troy this time, men," Herrod remarked when they were out of earshot. "I've waited too long to muff a chance like this."

CHAPTER FIFTEEN

AVALANCHE OF DOOM

WHITEY CRADE WAS LOAFING AT THE CHUCK WAGON with the riders gathered there for noon grub when Herrod had visited the camp to select four riders for his lynching, party. His first act had been to order Crade to cut a horse from the cavvy and report to the trail boss for duty.

Having ostensibly hired out as a Lazy H drover, the sullen albino made haste to comply, roping a strawberry roan from the string assigned to him by the wrangler and leaving camp at a gallop.

Always quick to offense, Crade had already made a bad start with the Lazy H crew. He resented their joshing remarks about his battered face and swollen hands, attributing his beating to some jezebel at Straight-Edge Lulu's house in Ruby.

109

As always, the colorless hair and skin of the man attracted cruel stares from normal men, and the Lazy H bunch had been no exception. They regarded him as a freak, and he knew it. All of Crade's life-long complexes and frustrations rode his shoulders as he reported to the Lazy H trail boss down the line and was assigned an outrider's position between the herd and the river.

When he found himself alone, with stragglers to beat back into the herd with a knotted rope-end and a definite purpose to occupy his attention, Crade shrugged the chip from his shoulder and turned the bitter spotlight of self-condemnation upon himself.

He had killed Del Troy. That conviction had become a part of him. He had never taken a human life before, and the enormity of his sin put a festering panic in the man which he knew no lapse of time nor ocean of liquor could ever expunge.

Reaction from his all-night vigil at Lily Basin and a head-splitting hang-over from his whisky debauch put his nerves in a state of near-collapse.

Troy's ghost rode at his stirrups. He heard Troy's voice above the clacking horns and beating hoofs of the herd lumbering in bovine stolidity alongside him. He saw Troy's face etched in the fumerols of dust which swept toward him from the green river, bringing its smell of rotting mud and tules, reminding him of Texas. Old memories marshaled to haunt him, and tears began to cut their salty swaths through the grime which hid the yeasty pallor of his face.

He screamed aloud, and the echo was a mockery lost in the rumble of the herd. The cattle were moving steadily up the bench, strung out in a tenuous column for three miles behind him. The country was flat and open, requiring little vigilance on the part of the drovers. He counted himself lucky that the trail boss hadn't assigned him to the dust of the drags. It did not occur to Whitey Crade that Bix Herrod had had an ulterior purpose in sending him out of camp ahead of the other cowboys.

He tried to roll a smoke but his hands were palsied and only after repeated tries did he manage to get a shapeless lumpy cylinder between his scabbed lips. He reined up to strike a match, and was grateful for the lift the nicotine gave him.

But gradually the heat and dust and noise put Crade under its sedative spell and he dozed, his mouth going slack. The cigarette dropped from his lips and fell unnoticed in the parched bunch grass behind his horse's hoofs. Instantly, ruddy flames flickered in the murk behind him like snakes' tongues, the smoke of kindling grass blending with the whorling dust.

Dreams took shape in macabre tableau behind Crade's lids. He dreamed as the roan drifted with the herd, knowing its duty and cutting a stray back into the main bunch without awakening its stupefied rider. Crade dreamed of another beef drive, in another year and on a remote range in the cactus flats of Oklahoma.

He dreamed that he was caught in a sudden stampede caused by raiding Comanche warriors, that he had been bucked from saddle and was helpless in the path of an oncoming tidal wave of hoofs and horns.

Behind him the grass fire spread, carrying the smell of smoke to the plodding steers.

Crade moaned in his sleep. He saw a tall rider angle like a phantom across the prairie between him and the stampeding Texas longhorns. The rider was Del Troy, whose unerring arm and rope sent release from certain death toward Whitey Crade, dragging him to safety at rope's end. That rope had linked them figuratively through the years, severed in a saloon brawl in Conconully.

The bawling of frenzied cattle loomed louder and louder in Crade's dream, until the dinning pressure of it against his eardrums was like nails being hammered into his skull; and the roar brought him screaming out of his dream, into the compounded horrors of a real stampede.

Fifty yards to the rear, the burning grass had already been beaten out by milling hoofs; but the damage was done and the Yakima pool herd, catching the scent of smoke and its mass panic spreading from animal to animal with the speed of a bullet's flight, had whipped the Lazy H and Dollar steers into a stampede.

Crade's horse, knowing the peril about to engulf them, swapped ends with devastating suddenness and arched its back like a ruptured clockspring, hurtling its rider into space.

Crade landed on hands and knees, and he felt the ground tremble under the strike of a thousand lethal hoofs as he staggered to his feet.

Yells thinned by distance and the sporadic pop of gunfire breached the hellish cacophony of bellowing cattle as other riders sought to head off the stampede and start the horned juggernaut to milling on the open plain.

Crade ran a dozen feet in a blind zigzag, making in the direction he believed the river to be, before a charging bull ripped open his side with a curved horn and flung the man to his belly.

Passing hoofs disemboweled Whitey Crade. His world became a blur of horned demons, knocking Crade down as fast as he tried to crawl away, dragging his torn

112

guts behind him. He smelled the acrid tang of his own blood as he went down for the last time under a thundering avalanche of doom.

The stampede spent its blind inertia after a five-mile run, Lazy H and Dollar riders keeping clear of the danger and compacting the herd with consummate skill. The cause of the stampede would never be known; but when it was finished, ashen-faced riders broke away from the noon camp, scouting the hoof-trampled wake of the stampede in search of possible victims.

Shasta Ives, no stranger to rangeland tragedies such as this, rode with the crew, investigating mangled carcasses of yearlings and she-stuff that had been overwhelmed by the juggernaut, making sure that no shapeless mass of broken bone and mangled muscle could be that of a luckless horse or fallen rider.

The cowboys swung north, relieved to find that the tidal wave of destruction had taken no human toll. Shasta reined back toward the chuck wagon, and quite by accident her eye was caught by a glint of sunlight on metal, far to the east where the benchland broke away into the Okanogan River farm belt.

Nausea touched her as she looked around for the other riders, but found herself alone on the prairie. She put her horse in the direction of the flash of light, impelled by a prescience that she would find death at its source.

Not until she was within a dozen yards of the shapeless heap amid the bunch-grass clumps did she realize that she had seen sun rays glinting on a belt buckle, and that the formless hulk in the dirt before her had once been a living, breathing human.

Shasta flung herself to the ground and ran forward, steeling herself for what she might find, stifling a selfish prayer that this would not prove to be one of her father's Dollar hands.

Only by the ruby-red irises of the half-opened eyes which regarded her was Shasta able to identify the stampede's victim as the albino pariah, Whitey Crade.

She was unaware that Herrod had put Crade on the Lazy H payroll last night, and the albino's presence here in the path of the stampede was a puzzle she did not try to fathom.

It seemed impossible, but life was not yet extinct in this mass of fractured bone and mashed flesh. Crade recognized her, calling her name through the blood which filled his lungs.

"I'm cashin' out one day too late," the dying puncher whispered, one ruined hand closing over hers as she knelt compassionately beside him.

"You'll pull through, Whitey," she lied, seeking to comfort his last moment on earth. "We have a skilled doctor riding with us. Mike Godette. He'll patch you up."

Crade shook his head ever so slightly, drinking strength from her taut smile.

"I shot Del Troy—this mornin'—south of Jones's Ranch," his rattly whisper reached her. "Killed the— only *hombre*—I could ever call friend. There ain't room in hell—for a man who'd—who'd—"

His whisper trailed off, and the impact of the albino's words took precious seconds to penetrate the girl's understanding.

"Crade! What are you saying? You didn't shoot Del Troy—I was riding that steeldust mustang this morning! You can't die without knowing that."

But the reassurance that he would meet his Maker without the stain of murder on his immortal soul came

114

too late to ease Whitey Crade across the Big Divide. His rabbit-pink eyes were fixed on Shasta's face when the torment ceased and he crossed beyond her aid.

CHAPTER SIXTEEN

NECKTIE PARTY

BIX HERROD HALTED HIS CAVALCADE ON A SPUR OF glacial rocks overlooking Horse Springs Coulee, near a surveyor's benchmark which indicated a point on the boundary of the Twenty-Mile Strip.

From this point, five hundred feet above the trail, the men with Herrod had an unobstructed vista of the Strip to its northern limits. Okanogan Jones's fortress-like ranch was a discernible dot against the sheen of Osoyoos Lake.

A spiral of dust moved against the diluted gray-green haze miles to the northward, visible only to the trained eyes of these range-wise men. Doc Godette unlimbered his brass telescope and focused it on the source of the dust.

"It's Troy," he reported, handing the telescope to Herrod.

Herrod studied the oncoming rider for some moments.

"We'll wait for him here, men," he decided. "Navet and McKnight, take a *pasear* down to that tamarack clump yonder and lie low. Fuller, you and Silva hole up in that rocky hump yonder. If Troy leaves the trail, signal. But I imagine he'll pass here."

The four riders moved off, grinning expectantly. Silva tripped around, balancing a Spencer across his

115

saddlehorn. "Troy's fair meat for any of us, boss?"

Herrod dismounted, handing the spyglass back to Godette. "No shooting. I want Troy to know who's counting coup on him. When he's boxed in, I'll give the word. I've already earmarked that cottonwood down there for Troy."

The horsemen moved off to vanish in their appointed lairs, bracketing the trail Del Troy was following. The sandy wagon tracks bore the recent hoofprints of two south-bound riders, Crade and Shasta. Herrod deduced that Troy would read the import of that extra set of tracks and follow them accordingly on the supposition that one set belonged to Shasta's ambusher.

Godette and Herrod led their horses into a brush-choked coulee and picked their way on foot down to the level of the road, seating themselves behind a jumble of bubble-pitted lava rocks under the shade of a gnarled cottonwood.

Herrod carried the coil of hemp rope with him, and his spatulate fingers set to fashioning the rope into the deadly five-roll hangman's noose.

"Bix, you got enough on Troy to hang him legal, with Shasta's testimony," Doc Godette commented between coughs. "I wouldn't put Troy's ghost between you this close to your weddin' day. I'd turn Troy over to Gaddy and let the law take its course."

Herrod, completing the noose to his satisfaction, coiled the rope carefully and set it aside. He bit the end off a Cuban cigar and studied Godette thoughtfully. During the years of his association with the ex-Confederate army surgeon, Herrod had usually followed the oldster's wise counsel, using Godette as a governor to counterbalance his own tempestuous judgments. But today he made his own stand.

116

"I'll tell Shasta that Troy started shooting and we were forced to drop him," he growled. "The girl's sharp. She'll get to wondering who cleaned off her wound, put that scarf on her neck for a bandage. Besides, there's Whitey Crade. That pink-eyed brockleface would spill Shasta an earful if I gave him half a chance."

Godette tugged the cork from his omnipresent bottle of rye and imbibed deeply, shuddering as the revivifying liquor warmed him.

"Crade must be disposed of *pronto prontico,*" advised the oldster, his voice taking on new vitality under the boost of the stimulant. "Yes, indeed. A most unusual physical specimen, that Crade. Rarely come across a true albino in the course of a lifetime's practice. I'd like to perform an autopsy on that one."

Herrod got his cigar drawing evenly and settled back for the long wait, grateful for the cottonwood's shade.

"You'll get your wish if Crade doesn't high-tail first," he said, fanning his face with his Keevil brim. "I can't afford to run the risk of Shasta talking things over with that maverick."

Godette fingered the tarnished brass buttons of his army tunic, letting his thoughts stray to other things.

"Shasta deserves a better deal than she'll get from you," he drawled. "A thoroughbred, that girl. And she trusts you to hell and back. You can't deceive her forever."

Anger glinted briefly in Herrod's eyes. "One thing you will not intrude upon, Doc," he said flatly. "My personal affairs. Always remember that. I've already taken more off you than any man living. Don't crowd me too often."

Godette turned his pale, wise eyes on his companion. "You cut a wide splash with most folks, Bix, but I've seen your cards and your bobtailed flush don't faze me a damn. Strong men are afraid of your strength and the weak ones kowtow to you the way weaklings will, hating your guts as they lick your boots. But I've had one foot in the grave too long to be buffaloed by the likes of you, Bix Herrod."

Godette watched Herrod's lips whiten, and it gave the oldster a perverse satisfaction, knowing his Svengali-like hold on the man, knowing the flaws as well as the strengths of the cattle king.

"I won't be around when Shasta gets wise to you," Godette went on. "You're on the top of the stack now. When you meet a better man, you'll cave, and drag Shasta down with you. Personally, I think you're waiting with that rope for the better man who might have coppered your bet."

It was a long speech for Doc Godette, and when he was finished Herrod made no comment, choosing to treat the oldster as he might a petulant child. Godette, having vented his spleen, turned over on his side and went to sleep.

The cottonwood's shadow had wheeled a considerable distance before Herrod shook the old soldier awake.

"Troy's abreast of the boys now," he whispered. "Skin out on the road yonder and tell Troy your hoss throwed you. Troy might go for his gun if we pulled a road-agent deal on him."

Doc Godette grunted and came to his feet. He yawned prodigiously, loosened the ancient Spiller and Burr percussion revolver in its scarred holster, and hobbled off around the boulder pile toward the road.

Crouched behind the bole of the cottonwood, Herrod waited with a cocked Frontier .45 in his fist.

Del Troy was less than fifty feet up the road, his jaded appaloosa mare limping from a thrown shoe. The Texan came erect in saddle as he saw Godette's shadow fall across the road ahead of him, his hand dropping instinctively to gun-butt.

"Make a habit of taking walks in heat like this, Doc?" Troy sang out, raking the roundabout slopes as he reined up, his eyes wary, alert.

"Bronc threw me tail-over-tincup and ran into the coulee yonder," the medico explained. "Thought you might dab your twine on the ornery jughead and save me a walk."

Troy remained tense, a warning tocsin ringing somewhere in the back of his head. "How come you were here in the first place?"

Godette gestured toward the uphill cairn marking the Strip. "This here's the boundary of Jones's range, son. Bix sent me ahead of the herd to scout the grass."

Troy's tension eased off slightly. He reached for his coiled lass'-rope. "I'll get your horse for you. Where is it?"

Godette started to gesture toward the mouth of a defile across the road. As he did so, a bluejay set up a chattering racket on a dead snag near by.

"See that jaybird yander, son?" Godette remarked. "Five gets you ten I can drill an eye plumb center, first shot."

As he spoke, Godette pulled the rusty Spiller and Burr from leather, twirling it innocently by the trigger guard. Troy saw nothing suspicious in the move, reading it as an old gaffer's pride in his marksmanship.

"I got my doubts if you could hit a barn door with a handful of corn," he grinned. "I'll take that bet, and double it if you knock a feather loose. Hell, that rebel blunderbuss won't carry fifty yards."

Godette bristled indignantly. He lifted the ancient piece, squinting down the sights. The bluejay scolded raucously, drawing Troy's eye toward the feathered target.

He realized his error instantly. When he jerked his head around to face Godette, the black bore of the gun was leveled at his midriff.

"Hold your fire, Doc!" Bix Herrod sang out from behind the cottonwood. "Reach, Troy. You're under a two-way drop here."

Caught, Troy groped his hands to hatbrim level as the massive figure of the Lazy H cowman stepped out from the roadside talus, sunlight glinting on a leveled Colt.

Godette, with a spongy chuckle, moved up with alacrity and jerked the gun from Troy's holster, following suit with the booted Winchester.

Navet and McKnight spurred out of the tamaracks behind Troy, joined almost immediately by Silva and Fuller from the rocky slopes above the road.

Troy, hearing the riders closing in behind him and reading the trap for what it was, grunted with self-disgust. "Always play it safe, don't you, Bix? This time you aim to make sure you finish what Fred Bolte started."

Bix Herrod waited until his four Lazy H riders had boxed Troy in from the real. Then he flung his hang-rope over the limb of the cottonwood and tied the slack to the trunk, leaving the noose dangling at a level which told Troy that he would be mounted when the lynch trap was sprung.

"Shasta beat your ambush up in Lily Basin this morning," Bix Herrod blustered, for the benefit of his men. "Lynch rope's too good for a man who'd draw down on a girl."

120

Troy got the picture then in its full perspective. He also caught a discrepancy in Herrod's words.

"Shasta doesn't know this country. How'd she know she was 'bushed in Lily Basin?"

Herrod bit his lip, aware of the slip he had made. His reference to Lily Basin had been a direct quotation from Whitey Crade's erroneous version of the bushwhacking of Del Troy.

"Rope him with his own reata, men!" Herrod ordered. "Let's get this business finished."

Silva and McKnight spurred alongside Troy's mare at the same moment, while Navet reached for the Texan's saddle rope.

Driving his spurs into the appaloosas flanks, Troy lashed a fist at Navet's jaw as the mare lunged forward. But the desperate bid for getaway was short-lived. Fuller drove in front of the mare to block its jump, and simultaneously Silva smashed his gun barrel at Troy's skull from behind.

His scalp gashed by the clubbing steel, Troy nearly toppled from saddle, fireworks exploding behind his eyelids.

He was vaguely aware of ropes pinioning his arms behind his back, trussing his elbows to his sides. Then Doc Godette led the mare under the dangling rope and Troy felt the scratch of hempen fibers brush his cheekbones and jaw as McKnight, spurring alongside him, fitted Herrod's noose around his neck with the roll snug to his left temple.

The stage was set for execution. Bix Herrod, whipping off his Keevil hat with a flourish, waved the riders back while he stationed himself alongside the appaloosa's rump. One swat of that hat would make the mare bolt out from under Troy, and the rope looped over the cottonwood limb would snap his neck like a twig.

But Herrod's arm froze at the top of its arc. It was a harsh command from Doc Godette, holding Troy's bit-ring, which caused Del Troy to open his squeezed-shut eyelids: "Hold 'er, Bix. You don't want your woman to see this."

Herrod wheeled about, his face losing some of its purple flush. Rocking around the south shoulder of the bluff came Shasta Ives, quirting a dead-beat Dollar cowpony up the road.

She bucketed to a dusty halt between Troy and Herrod, relief crowding some of the terror from her eyes. Thrusting a windblown lock of hair off her face, Shasta gasped out, "This is a tragic mistake, Bix. Whitey Crade ambushed me, not Troy. Crade told me with his dying breath."

Silva, obeying a signal from Doc Godette, reached to free Troy's neck from the noose as Herrod stared up at the girl.

"Dying breath? What do you mean?"

She told them of the stampede and Crade's ghastly end. When she finished Herrod said carefully, "Crade tell you why he tried to kill Troy?"

"No. Only that he regretted dying with his best friend's life on his conscience." Her glance touched Del Troy. "I'm sorry. He was gone before I could tell him it was a mistake."

Herrod had passed through the toughest crisis of his life, and his relief was evident in the slow exhalation he let leak through his lips. He saw Shasta turn to where McKnight was cutting Troy's bonds with a hunting-knife, and the moment the Texan's arms were loose she extended her right hand to him.

"Crade died because of me, Del. I shall never forget

that as long as I live. No amount of penance will ever free me of the knowledge that I wronged you so."

Troy massaged his chafed neck muscles and grinned slowly. "You just got through saving my hide, ma'am. I reckon that evens us up, don't it?"

Shasta turned to Herrod then.

"Not quite," she said grimly. "Bix, you lied when you promised me you wouldn't lynch Del. I'll overlook that. But I'm going to sign Crade's homestead over to Mr. Troy as soon as I can get to the county courthouse and draw up the necessary papers. The least I can do is put Troy back in full control of Flaming Canyon. I'm through being a pawn in your range-hog schemes, Bix."

For the first time since they had become engaged, Bix Herrod knew he was dangerously close to losing this girl who was so vital to his ambitions. He was realistic enough to know that eating humble pie in the presence of these men was his only recourse now, to salvage what he could of the girl's shattered faith in him.

"Of course, Shasta—I would have suggested turning the Crade place back to Troy if you hadn't. My abject apologies, Troy, for this necktie party. I let my temper get the best of me. Shasta claimed you ambushed her. I guess that made me a little crazy in the head."

Troy gave Herrod a strange, searching look.

"I don't suppose you know how Crade happened to be caught in a stampede of Lazy H cattle, do you?"

Troy's question warned Herrod that the Texan's mind was groping on the edge of a dangerous hunch, and he talked fast to divert him from the subject.

"Give Troy his guns, Doc."

When Troy had booted his Winchester and holstered his sidearm, he turned to Shasta Ives and lifted his hat.

"Your cattle hit the Strip today," he said. "Shasta, I'll

123

not object to your jag of Dollar beef grazing inside Flaming Canyon this summer, in view of what happened here."

He turned to Herrod then, and his voice sharpened.

"But I'll butcher the first mossyhorn I find on my grass with a Lazy H iron, Bix, and I'll shoot the first Lazy H hand I catch on my land. Let's get that straight, here and now."

Shasta laughed softly, the heat of anger still in her.

"Thank you, Del. I give you my word that Bix will not violate your lease with Okanogan Jones. It will cost him a bride if he does. There are limits to what I will do to make a dollar."

CHAPTER SEVENTEEN

SMOKE FROM METHOW

THE WORST DROUGHT IN WASHINGTON'S HISTORY, having scorched the Yakima rangeland into a tawny waste freckled with the bleaching skeletons of starved livestock, spread its blight northward as July ran its torrid course.

Washington's skies took on a perpetual brassy color from the haze of high smokes. Timber burned unchecked in the Mount Rainier area; farther to the east and south the golden wheat fields of Walla Walla and the Palouse withered before heading out.

The Okanogan country did not escape the searing hand of nature. Streams dried up to disconnected chains of mud puddles throughout the Twenty-Mile Strip. Only Flaming Canyon remained verdant, its cliff-shaded length irrigated by the seepage of Glacier Creek, which tapped the perpetual ice fields of the high Cascades to the west.

Snows receded on the higher peaks, leaving bald patches of granite. Okanogan Jones's timber cruisers reported that the fernbrake and hackberry undergrowth was tinder dry, needing only a careless camper's fire or a bolt of heat lightning to touch off a conflagration.

For Del Troy, July and the first two weeks in August were occupied with the herculean task of dismantling Okanogan Jones's sawmill in the upper Methow Valley, so that he was unaware of the drought which seemed to be dogging Bix Herrod's fortunes. He was engaged with the problem of stripping down a donkey engine's weight to a freight wagon's capacity when the driver of the Twisp stage dropped off a letter to him from Shasta Ives, postmarked Conconully.

It contained a quit-claim deed to Crade's homestead, made out in his name and accompanied by a hastily written note:

In view of the terrible drought conditions in the Strip, I have taken advantage of your kind offer and have had my men cut out all stock belonging to Dollar and put them inside Flaming Canyon. Naturally, I will reimburse you in full after the fall round-up.

Your fine steelduster, Alamo, is getting fat and frisky at Mr. Slankard's stable here in town and Miss Laranjo and I give him a workout every day to keep him in shape. Roxanna and I have become close friends since I took up residence at the Cariboo House. She thinks a lot of you, Del.

That was all; no mention of Bix Herrod, no reference to whether or not Lazy H beef had invaded the green reaches of Flaming Canyon during his enforced absence.

By August fifteenth, at the peak of the unprecedented heat wave, Troy had freighted the dismantled sawmill out of the Methow and delivered it to the site of Okanogan Jones's proposed logging-camp at the headwaters of the now dry Sinlahekin.

He sold the remainder of his mules and Conestoga caravan to the squaw-man, having no further use for them in view of Steen Slankard's retrenchment program, which Troy knew was preliminary to the trader's permanent withdrawal from the Okanogan mines.

He had better than a thousand dollars of Okanogan Jones's cash in his saddlebags when, after an eight weeks' absence, he alighted from the stage at Conconully.

It was like old times, seeing Ambie Pride crouched half drunk in the gutter in front of Beagle's Saloon.

"Well, congratulations must be in order," Troy laughed, helping the besotted oldster out of the dust. "What did the stork deliver, a heifer or a bullet?"

Ambie Pride grinned foolishly.

"That Jennie woman of mine is a contrary one," he admitted sheepishly. "Her baby ain't come yet. Any day now, Doc MacAdams says. But I could use the price of a dram in advance, to hold my nerves together when the ordeal begins."

Troy flipped the old tosspot a Canuck dollar and made his way over to the Silver Exchange Bank to deposit Jones's payoff to his account.

The gossip he picked up from the teller there was more encouraging than when he had left Conconully. The Arlington mines down at Ruby had resumed operations, as would-be Alaska goldseekers, discouraged over the difficulty of booking steamer passage to Skagway, had drifted back to their old jobs. Steen Slankard had sold out his Ruby store, but there was talk that the wily trader regretted having abandoned Ruby to oblivion so prematurely.

Although it was high noon, the blazing August sun was obscured behind a reddish haze which lay over the Cascades, filling Conconully's valley with a blanket of shadow similar to an approaching eclipse of the sun.

Troy passed up an impulse to saddle his mustang and make a jaunt over to Flaming Canyon to see how things were stacking up at his homestead. The past six weeks' labors had sapped his energy and he felt undisposed toward clashing with Bix Herrod in case he found Lazy H beef inside his lease.

Instead he went over to the Loop-Loop Casino and entered its welcome coolness. In the act of pushing through the batwings he had to step aside to avoid colliding with Roxanna Laranjo and Shasta Ives, who were carrying a bulging portmanteau between them.

"Del, *amigo*!" Roxanna was the first to recognize him. "You're just in time to see Shasta off for Seattle."

Troy doffed his hat, his gaze shuttling between the two women, struck by the comparison they presented—Shasta wearing a pert aigrette-feathered hat and a ribbed Marseilles bodice and traveling-skirt; Roxanna decked out in a rainbow-hued Mexican gown which accentuated the lovely curves of her body and complemented her dusky skin.

"Leaving us for the city, ma'am?" he inquired impersonally, stooping to pick up Shasta's luggage. "Can't say as I blame you. Puget Sound will seem mighty cool and green after this heat."

Shasta looped her arm through his as they headed out of the Casino and angled across the ankle-deep dust of the street, to where a hostler was hitching a span of Morgans to the Puget Sound stage. For the first time this summer, Guff Latchskin's coach did not have a capacity load of miners heading for the Klondike.

"I'm rigging up a cattle deal in Seattle," Shasta explained, after Guff Latchskin had deposited her baggage under the canvas curtained rack behind the Concord. "There isn't time to give you the details, Del. I'll leave that to Roxie here. And I hope you won't think I'm chasing a wild goose."

Latchskin's whip cracked and the stage jounced out of town with dust cascading from its spokes. Troy was aware of a vague sense of disappointment when he returned Shasta's wave.

Back in the Casino, sharing a jug of cool beer across Roxie's blackjack table, Troy waited for the lady gambler to open the conversation. He felt toward this strange, exotic woman an even stronger sense of kinship now, knowing he was forever in her debt as a result of her blocking the Keyhole to Lazy H cattle.

"You're wondering how a lady of Shasta's breeding could become the *compañera* of a gambling-hall hussy, *no es verdad?*" Roxie accused him half-seriously.

"Not at all. They don't come any finer than you, Roxie. There can be no thought of Shasta condescending to accept your company. I have no doubt she feels privileged."

Roxanna's statuesque shoulders lifted and fell in the expressive gesture common to her people.

"Outside of Jennie Pride," she smiled ruefully, "there are no women in Conconully to whom Shasta could turn for companionship. It was not my wish that she should seek me out in a—a hovel such as the Casino. It reminds me how low I have fallen."

128

Troy made wet rings with his beer glass on the green baize, suddenly ill at ease. He changed the subject.

"What kind of a cattle deal could take Shasta to Seattle this time of year? She'll have no difficulty marketing her beef this fall, what with Seattle jammed with gold hunters."

Roxanna fingered the wedding ring and the small gold cross on her neck chain.

"It goes back to that time she listened to a Klondiker talk about twenty-dollar beefsteaks in Dawson," Roxanna said "You were there, Del. It was at Okanogan Jones's place."

Troy laughed, recalling the forgotten incident.

"Good Lord, Roxie! Is Shasta still thinking she can drive a trail herd overland to Dawson? The gold rush will be petered out before she could get halfway across British Columbia."

Roxanna Laranjo shook her head.

"There are steamships operating between Puget Sound and Alaska. Shasta has the idea that she can sell her cattle to one of these shippers, at three times what the Seattle packeries will pay on the local market. I think she is on the right track. Those Alaska miners are hungry for fresh beef."

Troy rolled and licked a cigarette, his eyes thoughtful. "I doubt if any coastal steamer is equipped to handle a cargo of livestock, frankly. Not when the Seattle wharves are jammed to overflowing with tenderfeet willing to shell out five hundred dollars apiece for passage to Alaska."

Troy's eye strayed to the ring looped over the girl's necklace, and a new train of thought hit him.

"You'll be Shasta's maid of honor at her wedding soon."

129

Roxanna tucked the ring back under her dress.

"Del, I would not give odds that Shasta Ives will ever become Señora Herrod. He has not been to see her once since he set up his cow camp in the Twenty-Mile Strip. Does that sound like their love affair is prospering?"

Troy became aware that his pulses had picked up their tempo and he spoke hastily to cover his wonderment at that.

"How you women bandy gossip! Herrod's got his hands full keeping his Lazy H stock alive, I reckon. And you forget he has his eye on Dollar. He'll go through with that marriage to get it. I wouldn't sell his wedding day short, *querida.*"

They were silent for a long time, occupied with their own thoughts. A quarrel flared and died at a poker table near by without drawing them from their bemused reverie.

Roxanna spoke suddenly, bringing Troy back to reality. "You have known me many years, *amigo.* In Texas and Dodge City. You must be curious about this wedding ring I carry."

He shrugged, embarrassed without quite knowing why. "It is no affair of mine if you are a married woman, Roxie. I have always known there was nothing in the cards for you and me."

She caught his callused hands between her own, and in her eyes Troy read a wistfulness and a yearning which made him turn his head aside, as if he had seen her soul bared naked before him.

"You know that my religious faith denies me the divorce which my gringo sisters are free to use," she whispered. "Perhaps one day I will share a sordid story with you, *amigo.*" Her black eyes clouded forebodingly. "I feel I shall never see Chihuahua again, Del. I would like to know that this ring I carry could pass into your hands when I am gone."

He laughed then, uneasy before the morbidity that had crept into her voice.

"Shucks, *paloma mia*—you'll dance a fandango on my grave. You're fat and healthy—well, healthy anyway And you can't be over twenty-five. This kind of talk is not like you, Roxie."

She shrugged again, and the mood passed, leaving her face veiled behind the inscrutable mask she showed the world. A pair of muckers with the grime of the drifts on their rough clothing approached her table, grinning with the easy camaraderie of the time and place.

"How about some twenty-one, Roxie? Silver King opened today. We're aimin' to celebrate."

Roxanna Laranjo reached for her deck of cards, and Del Troy excused himself and left the Casino. His conversation with the girl had dulled the zest of his homecoming, and he crossed to Beagle's Saloon to hoist a few drinks with Ambie Pride, in hopes of shaking off his melancholy.

Dusk came prematurely, an hour before the sun touched the fir-clad hills west of the town, and it was dark enough for the kerosene flares to be lighted on the awning of the Casino when Troy went back onto the street. There was a smoky, resinous tang in the air that put a grim foreboding in the Texan, but he was too preoccupied with his moods to inquire into the reason for it.

Wheels rumbled out of the timber to westward, the twin eyes of oil lamps marking the eastbound stage pulling in from the coast. The Concord halted before Beagle's place and discharged a half-dozen miners returning to Conconully after an abortive visit to Seattle, the so-called gateway to the Alaska gold-rush. Scraps of their talk reached Troy as he watched the hostler changing the stage team for the run to Brewster:

"Five hundred bucks for standin' room in the hold of a stinkin' tub! And the same boat unloaded a thousand men who claim the Klondike boom is already busted."

"We may not get more'n day wages in the Okanogan diggin's this winter, but by damn we'll eat."

"They say the ice gits five foot thick on the Yukon by Christmas. A man's a fool to try his luck above White Pass any later than June."

Old man Beagle left his post-office annex, dragging a sack of outgoing mail. The stage tooler, tossing the Conconully mailbag down from the boot, remarked, "Damned near didn't get here this run, Beagle. Biggest forest fire in forty year is sweepin' through the Methow Valley toward the summit, faster'n a man can gallop a hoss. Liked to singed the hair outen my ears before I hit the east grade."

Del Troy's nostrils savored the thick, cloying fumes which choked the atmosphere and he knew a pang of quick alarm.

"That's smoke from Methow, eh?" Beagle grunted, shouldering his mailbag and express box. "Any danger the wind'll carry that fire down the foothills and wipe us out?"

The stage driver picked up his leather ribbons and kicked at his brake pedal.

"Anything could happen, Beag. I reckon by now Twisp is blazin' like a furnace. This dry weather's made a damned tinderbox out o' the mountings hereabouts. I'll be glad to cross the river."

Troy stepped down off the porch and yelled up at the driver, "Did you pass the Seattle stage this afternoon, Shufelt?"

The driver spat a gobbet of tobacco juice at a square lamp and the hot glass gave off a sizzling sound.

"Didn't I, now? Augered for ten minutes trying to make that knothead Guff Latchskin turn back. Told him it'd be like toolin' a stage into the devil's kitchen in hell, tryin' to cross the Methow with that fire gainin' ground like it was. Bet you any amount you want to name Latchskin don't git through. He'll fry in his own grease an' his passengers with him."

The Brewster stage lurched forward to the crack of Shufelt's whip. Troy paused a moment, indecision in him, then he headed past Slankard & Company's corral at a run and within moments was tossing a saddle onto his steeldust mustang.

Slankard was grooming a chestnut colt in the next stall. He had not seen Troy since the latter's return and he was chock-full of news.

"You hear about me buyin' a couple steamships for my lumber trade, Del? Auctioned off by the sheriff over at South Bend. Got 'em for ten thousand apiece, and worth a hundred. I aim to—"

Troy led his horse out of the stall, his face gray with strain. "Forest fire spreading beyond the ridge, Steen. Shasta Ives was on the noon stage. I aim to see if I can help. Shufelt thinks they're trapped."

Del Troy vanished in the darkness before Slankard could reply. Later, back in his office, Sheriff Gaddy arrived for their evening game of checkers and noted the depression which filled his crony. The lawman waggled his head slowly when Slankard told him about Troy's ride.

"We'll never see Troy again," Gaddy predicted, and a deep sense of loss put its hard pressure on the sheriff's lips.

CHAPTER EIGHTEEN

RED HELL

THREE HOURS OUT OF CONCONULLY, SHASTA IVES accepted the stage driver's invitation to share his topside seat, glad to quit the stuffy confines and dubious comforts of the Concord's interior.

The smell of smoke had become increasingly pronounced as the stage climbed the long grade up the foothill divide which marked the rampart of Methow Valley. Sundown found them still short of the summit when Guff Latchskin swung his Morgans out on one of the turn-outs of the single-track road, to let the inbound stage from Seattle pass.

The whiskered reinsman aboard the hurricane deck of the other Concord brought his thorough-braced vehicle to a dusty halt alongside Latchskin. Gaunt-faced passengers peered out at Shasta from the canvas-curtained windows.

"Slash fire over Twisp way has spread across the lower end of the valley, Guff. She's headin' north along the crown growth like an express train. You can't get through."

Guff Latchskin pared himself a quid from the twist of long green Missouri leaf he carried in a hip pocket.

"Been expectin' a burn this summer. How far below Twisp did this thing start?"

"Neighborhood of Old Goat Mountain, this side Lake Chelan."

Latchskin scoffed, unwinding his reins from the whip-stock. "I'll make it through, then. That's all of thirty mile."

Shasta saw the other driver eye Latchskin with obvious gravity.

"What I'm tellin' ye, Guff, is to get that junk wagon o' yourn turned around and foller me back to Conconully. By the time you hit the relay station at Twisp, the hull damned world will be a lake o' fire an' brimstone. I tell you, this one's a heller."

Guff Latchskin was a stubborn man and to him the greatest pride in life was maintaining his stage schedules. His face distorted by the giant chew he had tucked under his cheek, the jehu whispered a reassuring aside to his lady passenger: "Old Shufelt's ascairt of his own shadder, ma'am." Then, raising his voice, he addressed the other driver.

"Rattle your hocks, tillicum. I got a schedule to keep. By the time that fire covers the country between here an' Old Goat, I'll be eatin' supper west of the pass."

The Conconully-bound driver eyed Shasta worriedly.

"Better climb aboard with me, lady. This is the last chance Latchskin's got to turn his outfit between here and the valley bottom. I wouldn't like to see ye fry on account of Guff's dang-fool pigheadedness."

Before Shasta could voice an opinion, the Concord under her lurched violently on its bullhide springs and Guff Latchskin was hitting the summit grade, rocketing his vehicle around hairpin turns with reckless abandon.

"Like I said, that old yahoo tells everything scary, ma'am!" Latchskin chuckled, confident of his own judgment. "The forest fire ain't made yit that these Morgans couldn't outrun. A little smoke won't hurt us none."

They topped the divide and teetered down into the Methow in the face of a blast of super-heated air which made the team trumpet with panic and forced the girl to

135

shield her nostrils with a handkerchief.

Before they had put a mile of the steep switchbacks behind them, the surrounding forest was obscured behind a void of sluggish smoke and the black sky was laden with flying sparks and pine needles torn from the crown growth by the forced draft of the fire which was sweeping up the valley.

She sensed that Guff Latchskin had overplayed his hand when she saw the gaunt reinsman brace himself against the footboard and lash his Morgans into a run, which threatened to capsize the jouncing Concord at the steep, unbanked turns.

Shasta judged that they had skidded halfway down the valley grade when she caught sight of the first ruddy flash of flames eating up the declivity below the stage road.

Almost simultaneously a giant, centuries-old Douglas fir directly ahead of the stage exploded into flame, its resinous needles flaring like a two-hundred-foot torch, stripping the tree to a charred skeleton within seconds.

The furnace blast of the air was rapidly becoming unendurable to human lungs as the oxygen was sucked out of it. Shasta screamed in the driver's ear, imploring him to stop the team, but her words were lost in the funneling bass roar of the holocaust.

Latchskin was trying to stop the Morgans, she realized next. But the team was out of control. Whipsawing lines could not slow the stampeding animals, racing blind down a ten-degree slope. Latchskin's boot rode the brake lever, the locked wheels screaming in and out of ruts.

Then an elbow bend in the road loomed through a momentary rift in the whorling smoke clouds and Shasta knew, even as did Guff Latchskin, that their momentum would make it impossible to negotiate the turn safely.

"Jump fer yore life, lady!" Latchskin bawled against her ear. "I guessed this thing wrong—"

She flung herself out into space even as the careening stage left the ruts. Sheer luck carried her free of the pounding wheels and she hurtled head-over-heels into a yielding barrier of wild rhododendron scrub under the roadbed's rim.

Scratched and bleeding, she gained her feet in time to see the Seattle stage up end as its running-gear straddled a giant rock, the team breaking clear of the wagon tongue and sprawling in a tangle of harness to vanish in the smoke coils which hugged the slope.

The stagecoach disintegrated into slivers. One six-foot wheel, its axle gouged into the dirt, spun crazily through the smoke, spokes shuttering in the red witch-glow which filled the night. The screaming of mangled horses reached the girl's ears faintly above the organ-roar of the forest fire which was now advancing in an unbroken horseshoe curve below the road.

Discarding the ruins of her aigrette hat, Shasta brushed back her tousled hair and scrambled to the road's level. A blazing tamarack twig struck her, knocking her off her feet; her skirt was flaming when she got up again and she ground a handful of dirt against the charring fabric.

She staggered aimlessly in circles, her sense of direction lost in this inferno. The crackle of nearing flames blotted out the sound of her own screams as she called Guff Latchskin in the chaotic moments which followed.

Fire was leaping in recurrent waves up the mountainside, falling back and surging closer to the road with each wave. She made her way down to the smashed stage, breasting a tangible wall of heat, and knew then that she was alone in this lost world.

Latchskin, his skull skewered by a sundered bolster rod, lay wedged under the wreckage of his coach.

Terror lent its strength to the girl as she clawed her way back to the road. A rattlesnake slithered across her hand; a magnificent bull elk, flushed from its habitat by the advancing fire, bounced in forty-foot arcs up the hillside in defiance of gravity.

Instinct told her to crawl on all fours, where the air was purest close to the ground. The heat was singeing her hair now and she knew that death would probably come from suffocation before the flames actually touched her body.

Knotting a handkerchief about her nose and mouth, she fought her way up the road, following the zigzagging ruts while the thick undergrowth on both sides of the right of way smoldered, fumed briefly, then burst into open flame.

By what miracle of endurance she managed to reach the summit, the girl never knew; but the smoke thinned there in the face of a night breeze and the main body of the fire was behind her.

Utterly spent, she flung herself headlong on the hoof-trampled dirt and tried to choke the smoke out of her lungs.

Her ears had long since lost their function, stunned by the hellish roar of the holocaust which was the Methow Valley. A drowsy ennui filled her brain. The dust felt soft to her cheek.

This is what death is like, she thought, and drew comfort from its approach, welcoming its release.

The nightmare faded and cleared, faded and cleared yet again; she had no way of knowing that hours had elapsed while she lay here. The fire, slowed by thinning timber, had surrounded her now; its red rim was an unbroken fence about her.

Her imagination began playing her tricks. A face floated in the trembling heat waves which covered the roadbed, arid she knew it should be the face of Bix Herrod, her fiancé. But instead she conjured up the strained features of Del Troy, and it seemed to her that he was astride Alamo, the steeldust mustang she had come to regard as part of her life in Conconully this summer.

"The driver—the stage—how far beyond are they, Shasta?"

It was Del Troy's voice, and it sounded real enough, not like a figment of her deranged imagination, here on the portal of eternity. Strong arms were encircling her waist, lifting her; but even then she could not comprehend that Troy was actually here beside her, flesh and bone, not a ghost out of the red hell that engulfed her world.

"He's dead. Coach off the road. There's only me."

She was in saddle when she opened her eyes again; Troy's arm, its sleeve charred and blackened by the fiery gauntlet he had run, was supporting her body. The Texan, his face masked now with a bandanna, was spurring the steelduster off the stage road, down a brush-choked gulch on the far side of the summit which the fire had not yet ravaged.

Deluging sparks jumped the divide and the walls of the defile they were following showed patches of livid flame in scores of places as Troy sent the mustang hammering down the rocky notch.

The roar of the forest fire was an ocean breaker curling over them, enveloping them, as Troy slid off the mustang's crupper and hauled Shasta out of saddle.

Vaguely through the smoke she saw the black maw of a prospect hole looming against the granite face of the gulch; and Troy was driving the steelduster ahead of them up the sprawl of weed-grown mine tailings as he carried her in his arms like a child, his spike-heeled cow-boots grinding into the fractured rock for footing.

Fifty feet back in the semi-darkness of the abandoned mine tunnel Troy laid the girl down, and she licked the moisture which slimed the mossy rocks with her tongue, I greedily sucking the dank seepage through her lips.

The air was distilled ozone in this grotto. The silhouette of the horse stood guard like an ebony statue against the sullen red glare of the fire which had pursued them, like a disgruntled foe, to the very mouth of their sanctuary. "We'll be safe here," he told her, soaking his bandanna in a stagnant pool and swabbing her singed eyebrows and blistered cheeks. "Another five minutes and we'd have been barbecued like a leppie calf on a spit. You showed sense, staying on the road."

She rolled over on her back, the man kneeling beside her, massaging her throbbing neck and arms with the damp cloth. Her hands sought his and above the trembling violence of the flames roaring outside the mine drift, he caught her hoarse words.

"I was thinking of you there at the end, Del. Queer, isn't it? Funny that you should have found me, instead of Bix. But I—I'm glad."

Sleep came to her then, and it seemed that she had hardly closed her eyes when the weltering rays of an afternoon sun shafted into the mine tunnel and found her there alone. Troy and the horse were gone.

A momentary panic seized the girl, realizing how long she had slept. She scrambled her way to the mouth

140

of the cavern, her bare feet slipping on the wet rubble which carpeted the drift.

A high wind had scoured the Washington sky clear of smoke during the morning, and as far as her eye could reach the mountain ridges smoldered in blackened ruin, once-proud forests reduced to fuming snags of charcoal, the head-high underbrush now leveled to a downy mat of hot, gray ash as fine as talc.

Hoofs struck an abrasive discord against the rocks above the prospect hole and she turned joyously to see Del Troy stepping out of stirrups. His clothes were in rags, his jaw covered with a metallic glint of stubble like fine rusty wire. Here was a man who had gone through a literal hell to reach her side; the full meaning of his saga was something she would never learn from him.

"I've been up to the summit," he told her. "I'm not sure we'll find Conconully standing when we get back, Shasta."

"The fire was that bad?"

He made an elaborate business of fashioning a cigarette, keeping his eyes on his work,

"The Twenty-Mile Strip is a bonfire right now, I know that. The wind pushed the fire north and east toward the Indian reserve. I doubt if the river will stop it. This thing won't end until the first snow flies in November."

She pondered his report, realizing how it touched both of their destinies.

"Flaming Canyon will have lived up to its name, then. And I suppose Bix's cattle and my own are doomed."

He lighted his smoke from a glowing manzanita twig, and he made no attempt to minimize the enormity of the disaster which had struck the Okanogan country during the long night past.

"I wouldn't gamble a plugged nickel on finding that more than a handful of stock lived through this fire, Shasta. The way it looks from here, Okanogan Jones has been cleaned out. Fire is no respecter of man's ambitions."

She glanced at him with an altered expression, suspecting that he was thinking of Bix Herrod; but he was staring off at the smoking, black vista of the lower slope, the grim shape of his jaw telling her nothing.

"You and I are safe, Del," she said huskily. "Right now, I'm selfish enough to feel that that is all that counts."

His eyes swung full upon her then, and for a moment they held their wordless communion. And without either of them moving of conscious volition, they found themselves melting in a tight embrace, oblivious to all else around them.

Troy's mouth sought hers hungrily, demandingly, and long-pent hungers flamed through his blood with a healthy abandon as he felt her response.

He released her finally, reluctantly, and held her at arm's length, searching her eyes for some trace of remorse, but finding naught but a transcendental happiness there which matched his own.

It seemed to Del Troy in that moment that through the years behind him, his soul had been pointing toward this time and this place out of all eternity.

He dropped her arms, and something caught in a tatter of his sleeve. As she freed her left hand, both of them saw that it was Bix Herrod's Tiffany-set diamond which had snagged his shirt, as tangible a reminder of the gulf between them as if Herrod had suddenly materialized at their side.

He turned away, his face clouding as he realized how

142

things stood; that the promise of this thing which had come briefly between them was something false, a mutual yielding; that his dreams were empty, founded on nothing.

"We'd better ride," he said roughly. "I'd like to know what happened to Conconully."

CHAPTER NINETEEN

THE FRUITS OF PERFIDY

A SPARSENESS OF TIMBER FURRING ITS ROUNDABOUT slopes saved Conconully and the adjacent mines from destruction. The fire, following the conifers like flame traveling along a dynamite fuse, swung north after breaking out of the Methow Valley and roared across the Twenty-Mile Strip like a monster from the Apocalypse.

It paused to lick up the blockhouse and barns and bunkhouses of Okanogan Jones's citadel on Osoyoos Lake, hurdled the Canadian border, and swept its unleashed swath of red ruin on into the Rockies, where it would burn until the winter rains came.

For generations to come, the face of the Okanogan country would be scarred beyond recognition. Primeval stands of pine and alder, hemlock and fir were gutted out overnight, leaving a black and smoldering waste where charred snags jutted to the sky like bristles on an old brush.

Rumors filtered out of the smoke, speculation was rife; somewhere between them lay the truth. Okanogan Jones and his squaw Tenas Josie, so the report went, lost everything but the buckskins on their backs, and the log raft on which they escaped to the shielding embrace of Osoyoos Lake.

Bix Herrod and Doc Godette arrived in Conconully with the news that the Lazy H beef herd had been too scattered to drive to the safety of the riverbottom. Two or three Lazy H riders were so far unaccounted for. Herrod, like Okanogan Jones, was wiped out.

Del Troy left Conconully two days after his return with Shasta Ives, on an exploratory junket of his own. He found that out of all this smoking, tormented land, only Flaming Canyon had escaped the ravages of the fire.

Perhaps half of his leased range was consumed, but the bulk of the Canyon, including his homestead and Roxanna's place at the Keyhole, was far removed from threat of a new outbreak.

Paradoxically, Flaming Canyon's towering obsidian walls had shielded the verdure they embraced. And the cattle which had grazed on Troy's lease were safe, having followed the cool reaches of Glacier Creek out from under the flames which hurdled the rimrocks.

Troy spent one entire day making a tally of the stock on his leased graze. Five hundred and fifty-odd head of Dollar steers, a bare score of Lazy H beef had come through the disaster unscathed.

Outside the sunken course of Flaming Canyon, the picture was one of stark ruin. The air was a stench compounded of the fumes of roasted animal carcasses bunched in charnel pits at the ends of gullies and in box canyons. Herrod's cattle were mixed with the charred remains of deer, elk, rattlesnakes, jackrabbits, gophers, field mice—all manner of wild life from the regal panthers of the high slopes to the polliwogs of evaporated ponds had been cremated on the bier of the

144

Okanogan hills.

During an all-day scout of the Strip, the only signs of life Troy encountered were the scavenging flocks of buzzards overhead and a few Lazy H riders who were combing the brakes for their missing saddle mates.

Nature had extracted a bitter tax from Bix Herrod. Overnight, the Yakima cattle king, with his dreams of dominating Washington State's livestock industry, found his assets reduced to zero.

Sharing Herrod's fall from glory was Okanogan Jones. The king of the Strip was bankrupt, the monarch of a gutted kingdom of charred trees and stripped canyons and seared meadows. Nothing short of the eternal rocks had endured this fiery Armageddon. The earth had been blistered to its bedrock bones, leaving desolation in place of fertility, despair and defeat in lieu of the golden promise Jones's wide domain had held for his issue.

The sawmill which Troy had moved to the logging camp on the Sinlahekin was now a cooling mass of twisted, melted scrap. Okanogan Jones's dynasty had evaporated from the face of the earth, a burnt offering on the altar of Indian gods whose minions had once roved over this hunting-ground.

Del Troy returned to Conconully after spending a night with Okanogan Jones. He carried good news for Shasta Ives, the fantastic survival of her Dollar herd, and that errand alone made his return worth while from such a barren and sterile zone.

He expected to find Shasta at the Cariboo House, but as he tied up at the hotel rack he saw that the girl was conversing with her fiancé on the vine-hung porch.

It was the first time Troy had seen the Lazy H range baron since the hang-tree episode two months before,

145

and in that interim Herrod had aged perceptibly. Gray streaked his temples. He had lost weight and his well-cut fustian coat hung baggy on his frame.

The hatred which Herrod had once taken care to conceal when in the presence of his intended wife lay stark on the surface of the man now, plain to read in the hard strike of his eyes, in the lithic clamp of his mouth.

"You should be well satisfied with how things have turned out, Troy," Herrod greeted the Texan's arrival at the porch steps. "I lost twenty-five hundred head of prime beef because you kept me out of Flaming Canyon. I'll remind you of that one day."

Troy raised his hat to Shasta, ignoring Herrod. He wore no guns and he knew that fact relieved the girl.

"Bix has told you of your own good luck?"

The girl nodded, her mouth compressed, giving him the thought that he had interrupted a heated quarrel.

Troy shifted his gaze toward Herrod, wondering if the man's pride would yield enough to let him say some word of thanks for what Troy had done for Shasta Ives. But there was no gratitude printed on Herrod's face, only a consuming, festering hate which he made no effort to conceal.

Troy said finally, "Had I known this fire was coming, that it would jump my lease, I would gladly have invited you to throw your herd there, Bix. We're on equal footing now, you and I. Neither of us owns a calf to slap an iron on. Both of us are range poor. I'm willing to shake hands on a new start."

Herrod laughed harshly, his face twitching.

"You can go to hell, Troy. I hold you directly responsible for what Lazy H has suffered. I will have an accounting for that."

Troy tongued his cheek, keeping his feelings tautly

146

curbed. "That's how it stands between us, then?"

"Do I have to draw a picture for you?"

Troy shrugged. "*'Sta bueno,*" he said. "I don't offer my hand to a man twice." He turned to Shasta. "If you need me, I'll be glad to help haze your beef to Seattle this fall, Shasta. I imagine you'll need every drover you can rustle up."

Shasta had remained silent during the strained meeting of the two men, and she made no answer to Troy's offer as the Texan mounted and crossed the Salmon Creek bridge on his way to the Loop-Loop Casino.

From the hotel porch she watched Roxanna Laranjo emerge from the deadfall to meet Troy, and her face hardened under the stress of secret emotions as she watched them vanish beyond the square façade of the building.

"You should have shaken hands with Troy, Bix," she murmured. "He showed himself the better man today."

Herrod flushed, hitching his chair closer to the girl. His hand reached out to where hers lay in her lap, his fingers toying with the square-cut diamond solitaire he had given her.

"As I was saying, Shasta," he said with a humility that was rare in him, "a man needs a woman most at a time like this, when his world has crashed around him. I'm going back to Yakima tomorrow. We could be married by the mission padre over at Pateros on the way home."

Shasta pulled herself back to reality, staring at Herrod as if she had not heard him. "I'm not going back to the home ranch, Bix. It holds too many unhappy memories for me since Dad died."

He lit a cigar to bridge the awkward silence that built

147

up between them, and spoke around it, his voice brittle. "I'm not asking you to go back to Dollar. I'm asking you to be my wife. My credit's good at the banks. Together we can start out again, the two of us, and rebuild the Lazy H."

She got to her feet, picking up the straw sailor she had hung on the chair back and pinning it on her piled-up hair.

"Dollar is for sale, Bix. I'll accept a mortgage from you on your own terms. That's what you really wanted of me, wasn't it? Title to Dad's holdings in Natchez Valley?"

Fear was born in Herrod's eyes now, the fear of a man who saw the inevitable fruits of his perfidy ripening for the harvest. Doc Godette, an older and wiser man than he, had warned him against this eventual moment of rebellion from Shasta Ives. He knew now that he had lost whatever grip he had held on her heart.

"I love you, Shasta. I want to remind you that you are betrothed to me. Dollar does not enter into that."

He had said the wrong thing. He had given her an opening. She was steeling herself to voice a decision that had been a long time in shaping up in her mind. He knew that too late to rectify what he had said.

With a slow, cool deliberation, as if weighing the consequences of what she was about to do, Shasta took the diamond from her finger and thrust it into his palm.

"We're finished, Bix. Whatever affection I knew for you has died, as completely as death can be. I don't know when it happened. I don't want to be melodramatic about it now. I've always been honest with you, Bix. I don't feel you have been the same toward me. I feel you have used me as a pawn to further your own ambitions."

148

Herrod stared at the ring, then flung it savagely away from him. It struck the street with a little geyser of dust and the facets of its blue-white stone glittered in the sunlight like a drop of distilled brilliance, attracting a cruising insect.

"Del Troy has come between us."

Herrod's flat statement stung her, brought her wheeling to face him. Her eyes were dry, her breathing controlled. "Of course not. How dare you suggest such a thing?"

He said, "You can't deny he's made a play for you. Risking his hide to track down that stagecoach the day the fire broke."

"He saved my life. Perhaps I could love a man for that, if other things were equal. But if Del Troy has room in his heart for any woman, that woman is Roxanna Laranjo."

Herrod opened his mouth, then clamped it shut without saying whatever had come to his mind. He turned and stalked down the hotel steps and then, remembering something, wheeled back and from a pocket of his fustian coat took out a folded cardboard placard which he opened and thrust in front of her.

"Read this," he challenged. "It might make you change your mind about a few things."

She stared at the printed poster, the black and red type blurring through her tears. She recognized it as a duplicate of a sign she had seen tacked on the post-office bulletin board over at Beagle's that morning.

PUBLIC LAND SALE

Having decided to dispose of my extensive holdings in

the Twenty-Mile Strip as a result of the recent fire, all lands deeded in my name or that of my lawful spouse, Tenas Josephine Jones, will be placed on public sale at one dollar per acre on Friday, October first, at 9:00 a.m. All sales to be cash, subject to current taxes, existing liens, and easements under the law.

First come, first served. Lands available at this sale may be located on the plat of the Twenty-Mile Strip, available for public inspection in the archives of the Okanogan County Clerk of Records, Courthouse, Conconully, Washington.

CYRUS (OKANOGAN) JONES
Osoyoos Lake Ranch, Wash.

Shasta looked up, surprising a leer on Herrod's face.

"What does this have to do with my changing my mind about us, Bix? If you are inferring that my decision had anything to do with your loss of worldly goods—"

He waved her off. "If you take it as an insult, I apologize. No. Jones's sale means that Flaming Canyon will go to the first bidder who can offer Jones thirty-five thousand in cash. I could raise twice that on my equity of the headquarters ranch from any bank in Yakima."

"But Del Troy has a year's lease to run on Flaming Canyon. Jones couldn't sell that portion of the Strip."

"Couldn't he? Why not? When Troy's lease expires next year, a new owner would be under no obligation to renew his option under Washington law." His manner softened. "I'm offering you half interest in Flaming Canyon as a wedding gift, Shasta. Jones is out to salvage what he can from the wreckage of the Strip. When he was sitting tight in the saddle he feared and hated me. But he would sell Flaming Canyon to me

150

now. Make no mistake of that."

Herrod turned on his heel and headed down the steps. A screen door banged as Shasta Ives retreated into the hotel—and it gave Herrod an opportunity to search in the dust for his diamond ring without losing face. He recovered the gem and pocketed it, smiling with satisfaction.

He thought, *She'll come back to me on her knees,* and he headed toward the Loop-Loop saloon to drink on his prediction.

CHAPTER TWENTY

SINISTER EVENTS

IN THE PRIVACY OF A GAMBLING-BOOTH IN THE LOOP-Loop Casino, Del Troy told Roxanna Laranjo of Okanogan Jones's decision to abdicate his Twenty-Mile Strip throne.

The news that Flaming Canyon was available for purchase had brought mingled hope and despair to Del Troy, for it had come several years too soon. He knew from a study of government surveys that thirty-five thousand dollars would be the value Jones placed on the slightly less than fifty-five sections which the canyon encompassed from the Keyhole to the headwaters of Glacier Creek. A large percentage of this acreage was prime grazing land, even tillable in case nesters ever invaded it with hoe and plow.

It was a golden opportunity, one which Troy had not expected to see open up while Jones was alive. But the fire had wiped out the squaw man's timber, and he had no interest in farming or cattle ranching.

"This October first sale may see hundreds of sod-busters bidding for Flaming Canyon," Troy said at the outset of their tête-à-tête. "Herrod's broke, so I'm not worrying about him. But you know and I know that my homestead and Crade's would never make a cattle spread. It looks as if it took an Act of God to lick me, Roxie."

"No," the Spanish girl said. "You must buy what you can of the Canyon. If Señor Jones would agree to a long-term mortgage, you could own the entire Canyon, free of debt, inside of ten years. Beef will fatten there as nowhere else. And you have a market for all the beef you can raise, at the Indian agency."

He smiled bitterly behind curling cigarette smoke.

"I grant you that. But Jones is after cash. At a dollar an acre, I couldn't expect him to carry me."

"I have some dinero saved," she said earnestly. "The cards have been kind to me since I took up gambling. A tithe I have given to the Mother Church. But I have seven thousand pesos in the bank at Del Rio. It is yours for as long as you need it without interest."

Her generosity stirred him more deeply than he cared to admit, but he had his own pride and his own convictions.

"*Muchas gracias,* Roxie. But I cannot do that."

They left the Loop-Loop when a bell signal from Beagle's Saloon informed Conconully that the mail was ready for distribution, and Roxie accompanied him over to the post office.

A decided change had come in the weather after the month-long dry spell. The fire which had gashed a deep wound in the backbone of the Cascades had pulled rain clouds in from the Pacific and the Olympic Peninsula, and awesome thunderheads were racking up in blue-

152

black masses above the denuded summits west of Conconully.

Humidity weighted the air, making breathing difficult. A few warm drops of flat-swollen rain dimpled the dust, wept from the eaves of Conconully's buildings as Troy and Roxanna joined the group in front of the post-office annex.

"We're in for a good soaking," Sheriff Gaddy commented, scanning the ugly cloud formations. "A pity this storm couldn't have come in time to put out the fire. But after the fire cometh the deluge, the Good Book says."

Troy, sorting through a week's accumulation of mail, turned to Roxanna and said, "I think I'll pull stakes for the homestead before this storm breaks. When the weather lets up I'll take a pasear over to Jones's Ranch and see if he'll do business for less than cash on the barrel head. I doubt if I have any luck."

Roxanna gripped his hand, her heart's desire in her eyes. "Good luck, *amigo*. Remember what I told you— about my money. It is yours for the asking."

Troy left her then to get his horse and took the north road out of camp on his way to Flaming Canyon. Roxanna went back to her room for her afternoon nap. She covered her face with cloths soaked in skimmed milk, for her beauty was her chief stock in trade, her attractiveness ranking equally with her reputation for a square game to draw gamblers to her table.

She was dozing off when a knock sounded at her door and she arose to admit Shasta Ives. The girl thrust an envelope into Roxanna's hand, and excitement made her features glow.

"I wrote to the Alaska steamship people over in Seattle," Shasta said, "and I wanted you to be the first to read their answer. I accomplished as much by writing as

153

I would have done by a visit to Seattle."

Roxanna found a flint and wick and got a wall lamp going. Her jet eyes raced over the purple typewriting:

DEAR MADAM,

Your favor of the third inst. received and contents duly noted.

In reply wish to state that your proposal to ship live cattle to the Alaska market has been considered by our board of directors.

As a speculation, this firm is prepared to purchase up to 500 head of beef steers at three times the prevailing stockyard prices, or approximately sixty dollars per head delivered to our dock on Elliot Bay, Seattle, subject to customary inspection procedures of local abbatoirs.

Trusting to receive an early and favorable reply, we beg to remain, Madam,

Yr Ob't Servants,
ALASKA MARITIME CORP.

"You see, my dream was not so foolish after all, Roxie!" Shasta said exuberantly. "I still have enough of Dad's crew left to take my herd to Seattle. Del will serve as my trail boss. I must tell him this news. Just think, sixty dollars for a steer worth only twenty on the local market!"

Roxanna handed back the letter and pulled Shasta to her,embracing her affectionately, knowing how much this news meant to the girl.

"I'm afraid Del has already left for Flaming Canyon," she said. "And with a bad storm brewing, you will not want to ride after him. Come downstairs. Jodie, the bartender's little boy, will be glad to deliver your

154

message to Del."

In a darkened booth at one end of the Casino's barroom, Bix Herrod roused from a moody contemplation of the whisky bottle which had been his companion throughout the afternoon, his alcohol-flushed face fixing in a scowl, watching with keen interest as he saw Shasta Ives and Roxanna Laranjo descend the stairs and confer with the bartender. Borrowing a tablet, Shasta scribbled a hasty note.

Herrod was not too drunk to miss overhearing Shasta's instructions to Jodie, the thirteen-year-old son of the Casino's barkeep. Shasta was sending an urgent message to Del Troy.

To Herrod's distraught brain, that paper could carry but one item of news. Shasta was letting Troy know she had broken their engagement.

A seething, irrational anger took possession of the Lazy H cattleman as he saw Shasta leave the Casino on her way back to her quarters at the Cariboo House. He waited until Roxanna had returned upstairs to change her dress in preparation for the night's gaming, and then he emerged from the booth.

Incoming patrons buffeted Herrod as he approached the door but he elbowed them aside with a blind, miserable rage filling his veins. Rain was beginning to fall over the darkening street as Herrod lurched down the steps and headed toward the rear end of the Casino.

He arrived at the lean-to stable there just as Jodie, the bartender's son, was leading a saddled pinto into the open. With a savage gesture, Herrod snatched the folded sheet of paper from the pocket of the younker's linsey-woolsey shirt.

"Hey, Mister Herrod! I've got to ketch up with Del Troy and deliver that there paper—I'm getting two bucks for the ride."

Herrod cuffed Jodie aside, struck a match, and scanned Shasta's brief message, his contorted face gradually relaxing as he absorbed its context.

Friend Del:

Please return to town at once. I have extremely important news and must see you immediately. I will wait for you at Room F in the Cariboo House.

Yours faithfully, Shasta.

Herrod folded the missive and thrust it back into Jodie's pocket. He fished in his pants and drew out a gold coin, flipping it to the wide-eyed youth.

"This eagle is for keeping your mouth shut about me reading this paper, sonny. Take it along to Del Troy as Miss Ives told you to, savvy?"

Jodie crow-hopped into the saddle, his freckled face beaming under the steady dash of rain.

"Gee, Mister Herrod—thanks! You betcha. I won't talk."

Jealous demons pricked Herrod with their tridents as the Lazy H rancher returned to the main street and sought the shelter of Grainger's Gun-Shop porch, from which place he could see the lighted upper windows of the Cariboo House marking Shasta's private suite of rooms. Within the hour Del Troy would be keeping a tryst with the girl Herrod had planned to marry.

A form took shape beside Herrod and the scraggy paw of the town drunk, Ambie Pride, plucked his sleeve and extended a dirty palm.

"Got four bits to spare for a shot o' red-eye, Mister? My tongue's dryer'n a bootsole an' I got a two-mile walk home in the rain to where my woman's expectin' a baby any hour—"

Herrod flung the begger from him with an oath. Then, his manner suddenly changing, he helped Pride out of the mud and pulled him back against the clapboard wall of the gunsmith's. From a wallet Herrod took out a twenty dollar bill. He tore it in two, handing Pride one of the halves.

"You get the other half of this frogskin if you deliver a message to Shasta Ives over at the Cariboo, Ambie."

Pride pocketed the torn bill and rubbed his bony hands together suppliantly.

"For a double sawbuck, Mister Herrod, I'd cut my old lady's throat. What's this message?"

From the window of her room on the second story front corner of the Loop-Loop Casino, Roxanna Laranjo was staring out through the rain-lashed night while she counted off fifty strokes of a brush through her shimmering black hair.

Intermittent flashes of lightning flickered across the black heavens, throwing the battlemented store fronts of Conconully into sharp relief. The storm had driven men off the street, with the solitary exception of a man who crouched in the shelter of Grainger's shop across the street.

She was winding her hair into a glossy bun at her neck when a particularly spectacular burst of lightning showed her a second man abroad in the night. The drunkard, Ambie Pride, was sloshing through the mud to meet the man at the gunsmith's porch.

As the greenish glow of electricity tapered off, Roxanna recognized with a start that Pride was meeting Bix Herrod, and she mused on the strange reversal of fortune which should make the Lazy H tyrant stoop to consort with Conconully's prodigal.

The glare of a passing wagon's oil lantern showed Roxanna something which piqued her interest. Herrod handed the town drunkard an object, which Pride thrust into his pocket. Then, after shaking Herrod's hand, the drunkard headed for Beagle's Saloon and vanished inside.

The next time a bolt of lightning ripped across the zenith, the gun-shop porch was empty. Through the tail of her eye she glimpsed Bix Herrod crossing the Salmon Creek footbridge in front of the Cariboo House.

Putting the finishing touches to her primping, Roxanna Laranjo blew out her lamp and made her way downstairs into the stifling fumes of lamp oil and tobacco and cheap whisky which she must endure until the night's long chore was finished.

A hatred for all the tawdriness which surrounded her life came to the girl. She sized up the nude paintings over the gambling layouts, the unkempt miners lining the brass rail, the racked guns and moose heads and all the other accouterments of the saloon, and a revulsion passed through her.

She felt the need for a stimulant and paused to order a glass of claret sent to her table. As she was leaving the bar a draft touched her cheek from the street doors and Shasta Ives stepped into the deadfall. The girl's cheeks were flushed with excitement and she was wearing an oilskin slicker and a wide-brimmed Stetson that dripped rainwater.

"Shasta, you must not come in this—"

"I know, Roxie. But Ambie Pride just looked me up," Shasta said. "His Jennie's baby is coming at last. Doctor MacAdam is already on his way out to the Pride shanty. Ambie says the doctor wants me to help out."

A smile softened Roxanna's face. The pregnancy of

158

Ambie Pride's wife had been followed by this town with increasing interest for weeks.

"Roxie, I won't be at the Cariboo when Del gets back to town," Shasta went on. "Would you give him this Seattle letter for me when you see him, and explain what happened? I left a note pinned to my door, telling him to see you."

Roxanna took the envelope and thrust it into the bosom of her Spanish gown. *"Por seguro,* Shasta, dear. And I hope Señora Pride has a comfortable time tonight. My prayers go with you."

Roxanna watched from the saloon window as Shasta went out to her waiting horse and vanished in the slanting downpour, headed for Ambie Pride's shanty two miles up the gulch.

A rare exhilaration was in Roxanna as she went back into the congested end of the barroom and took her accustomed seat at the blackjack table. Her arrival was being impatiently awaited by five or six of her steady customers, and in a moment she was exchanging chips for specie.

The voices of the gamblers touched her abstractly; her thoughts were far afield tonight. "I'll stand." "Hit me easy. A jack! That busts me."

Roxanna's mind was not on the game. Her eye ranged toward the bar, impatient because her wine had not been delivered by the white-jacketed floorman.

Then her eyes suddenly widened, drawing a droll remark from one of her players. "You look like you're seein' a ghost, Roxie! Place your bet, Joe."

Roxanna was staring off across the smoke-shrouded room to where a group of miners were about to open a rondo-coolo game. With them was the Conconully doctor, Duncan MacAdam, stripped to his shirt sleeves and obviously settling down for a long play.

A cold premonition touched the girl as she dropped her deck of cards and stood up.

"I'll drop out this round, Señores—"

She crossed over to Dr. MacAdam's table.

"Señor Doctor! Are you not delivering Jennie Pride's baby tonight?"

A round of laughter circled the table.

"Ambie's been bragging again, has he?" laughed the medico. "No, Roxie. Take my professional oath on it, Jennie's time is still a week off. I will be on hand when the stork makes his appearance, you can bank on that."

A cold constriction went through Roxanna Laranjo as she turned back to her table. Sinister events were shaping up behind the storm tonight.

"Gentlemen," she apologized to her players, "this game is closed. I—I feel ill. I must cash in your chips and retire to my room."

CHAPTER TWENTY-ONE

A TRYST WITH DESTINY

IN THE PRIVACY OF HER ROOM, ROXANNA LARANJO removed heir low-cut scarlet gown and donned the austere black silk which she reserved for confessionals and holy communion.

A steely insouciance had claimed her. She moved like a puppet, like a sleeper in the coils of a nightmare. Intuition told her she had a tryst with destiny tonight. The mood sent her to her dresser where she kept her rosary, and her lips moved as she counted the beads for a prayerful moment.

From a camel-back trunk under her bed, Roxanna removed a rich mantilla of black lace with the scent of cedar oil on it. She draped the heirloom over her head and shoulders, and from the trunk she took a single-shot .41 derringer.

Thrusting the tiny weapon under her sash, Roxanna stepped out into the corridor and left the building by the outdoor stairs which served as a fire escape. No one saw the black-shrouded shape move through the dank gloom of the storm and cross Salmon Creek bridge. Bone-dry this morning, the shallow gravelly bed of the stream was alive with the secretive whisperings of rising waters now. She put the bridge behind her and slogged through ankle-deep mire toward the looming shape of the Cariboo House.

Avoiding the lobby entrance, Roxanna climbed the outside stairs and entered the black gut of the hotel's upper hallway. She paused a moment there, the gruff roil of thunder shaking the building, rain pounding the shingles overhead like flung pebbles.

Her hand sought the crucifix at her throat and her finger tips drew strength from the sacred talisman of her faith. She knew a moment's mortal fear, and rejected it. The fatalism of her race was a shield and a sustaining force for what lay ahead. Her damp dress clung with an adhesive sheen to the curves of her body, as she moved down the carpeted hall, wet skirts swishing.

A crack of lamplight spread fanwise under the door marked *F*. She saw the white rectangle of the note Shasta had pinned there for Del Troy; and she concluded that the girl, in her haste to answer Ambie Pride's call for help, had left her lamp burning.

The door was unlocked and Roxanna stepped inside, her face a marble oval behind the dripping lace veil. She

161

closed the door behind her with a muddy heel.

This was Shasta's living-room, pine-walled and austere in the mode of the frontier, furnished with ornate Victorian pieces. A pink hobnail lamp glowed under its green shade atop a writing-desk; chintz curtains closed off a door leading into Shasta's bedroom off to the right.

A faint odor of whisky and wet wool clung to the room, its thin effluvium telling Roxanna what she wanted to know.

Roxanna draped her mantilla about her, its dripping lace hiding her right hand as it sought out the tiny curved handle of the derringer under her sash.

Her black eyes fixed on the bedroom doorway as she spoke. "Come out of there, Bix."

Silence greeted her, to be broken by an ear-numbing clap of thunder reverberating like a giant's timpani over the storm-punished valley. A windowpane rattled in the bedroom. The gale moaned under a vibrating shingle somewhere on the hotel's eaves.

She waited, knowing she could not be wrong. Suddenly the chintz curtains moved, parted by a hand that held a Colt revolver. Bix Herrod stepped out of the bedroom, his eyes squinted in the lamplight, rain's recent dampness sparkling on his coat and leaking from the brim of his Keevil hat.

Drink and hate and suspense had twisted the man's face into a satanic grimace. "By God, Roxie, you've followed me too far this time."

He seated himself on a horsehair divan facing the girl, balancing the .45 barrel across one knee. Roxanna's pale lips moved behind her veil.

"You paid Ambie Pride to get Shasta out of town on a pretext. You know Del Troy is due to come here. You're waiting to murder him."

162

Herrod's teeth glittered under his shadowing mustache. He growled, "Shasta tossed me over for that Texan today. Gave me back my ring. If I can't have her, I'll make damned sure Troy doesn't either."

Roxanna had not known of this development, for Shasta's friendship had not reached that intimate a stage. but the news transformed the harsh planes of Roxanna's face, easing the tension there, flowing through her like cool air relieving a long fever.

Herrod spoke again, rubbing his stubbly jaw with a knuckle, his other hand hefting the Colt. "I'm going to kill you, Roxie. I've known I'd have to, ever since you turned up in Conconully. By God, you're—"

Herrod broke off, stiffening as he saw the glitter of a derringer muzzle behind the gossamer webbing of her mantilla.

"I won't let you ruin Shasta's life as you crucified me, Bix." She closed her eyes. "Mother of Jesus, forgive me—"

She shot him in the chest without aiming the derringer. The .41 slug caught Herrod in the act of springing to his feet and the drilling shock of it unhinged his knees, dropped him face forward, his own gun skidding across the rug in front of him.

He pulled himself up on all fours, like a sprinter crouched to start a race. Great ruby drops of blood leaked from his vest and trickled down his looping watch chain the fat beads swelling to fall free, the carpet's pile drinking them up.

Herrod was staring at Roxanna, his lips peeled off his teeth, a vast surprise in him.

"You she-lobo. You greaser witch—"

Gunpowder had ignited Roxanna's veil, the lace glowing red as the smolder spread. Its smoke filtered

163

across her eyes as she turned and reached for the doorknob.

Herrod's gun was within reach on the floor. With an effort that drained the color from his face, he scooped up the .45 and fought its dead weight until he had Roxanna's shapely back under his gunsights.

The heavy .45 roared and bucked against the crotch of Herrod's thumb. Through founting gunsmoke he saw Roxanna's shoulders jerk violently against her neck as the bullet smashed her high on the spine, lifting her on her toes.

The shock drove her forward against the door. One splayed hand sought the varnished casing, clutched it. She pressed her cheek against the wall for support, and then her head slid down the wall in slow jerks, her body twisting half around as she slumped. When she came to rest, her head was turned toward him. Her lovely eyes held no malice and no regrets as their brilliance slowly faded . . .

For a long moment Herrod stared at the woman he had killed, and there was no remorse in him, only a swelling sense of horror as he felt his own life spilling out.

Clutching the arm of the divan, Herrod pulled himself to his feet, listening to the roar of the storm which had covered the exchange of shots. He holstered his gun, instinct telling him it must not be left behind to betray his presence here to those who would discover this tragedy.

Doubled over with the cramp of his wound, Herrod pressed both palms over the welling blood which soaked his vest and made his way back into Shasta's bedroom.

Thunder and lightning played over the invisible hills above and around Conconully as Bix Herrod got a window sash open and straddled the sill. He half fell, half jumped to the flat slope of the hotel's back porch. Invisible down there was the ladder he had used to gain access to Shasta's rooms.

He skidded on the wet shingles and went over the eaves, the shock of his ten-foot drop cushioned by a mound of stovewood. Hitting the mud, the wounded cattleman writhed for a moment in his agony, then searched the slanting downpour for the misty blur of lamplight marking the uphill cabin where he and Doc Godette were living.

Godette had saved his life once before, in Texas. He was the only man in the world who could help Bix Herrod now.

CHAPTER TWENTY-TWO

SWEPT INTO LIMBO

THE STORM WAS ROARING TOWARD ITS CLIMAX AS DEL Troy and young Jodie headed back toward Conconully. Jodie had overtaken the Texan within a mile of his goal at Flaming Canyon.

What news Shasta Ives had for him, Troy could not guess. But the urgency of her short message was enough to keep his steelduster at a steady gallop, giving the horse its head through the Stygian gloom.

They reached the canyon of Salmon Creek where the road bent down-gulch toward the county seat, to find a shallow trickle of water instead of the gushing run-off which the storm should have brought from the burned-off slopes at its headwaters.

"The storm's tapering off, Mister Troy!" Jodie piped

up in his childish treble. "An hour ago when I crossed, the crick was withers deep to my paint hoss."

On the far bank, Troy reined up. The rain hammered his oilskins like pelting buckshot. Up-canyon he could hear a thunderous churning of angry waters, the wrench and grind of moving boulders, the splintering crunch of logs being snapped like toothpicks.

"No," Troy shouted to the bartender's kid. "This is bad. There's a log-jam up at the rapids most likely. If it had busted loose when we were crossing, you and I would have been drowned like rats."

Instead of reining south toward Conconully, Troy pushed up-canyon to investigate, Jodie following him with frightened wonder. When they reached the crest of the rise, a dazzling lightning burst blinded them momentarily and the acrid taste of raw ozone hit their nostrils. The lightning discharge had struck a snag dangerously close by.

The pinched-off glare revealed a scene of pure menace to Troy. The rock-ribbed gulch was brimming with congested waters, the creek's run-off temporarily blocked by the tons of boulders and uprooted trees which had jammed the narrow aperture of the rapids. When that backed-up lake let go—

Troy jerked the steelduster around and raked his spurs, flinging a desperate shout at Jodie.

"Flash flood coming up, Jodie. We've got to warn the folks in town. When that log dam gives way Conconully is li'ble to be wiped out—"

Jodie, bent low over his pinto, sobbed his terror as he hammered after Del Troy. They passed the looming shafthouse of the Silver King and skirted its tailings, galloped under the chute scaffolding which crossed the road and reached the outskirts of the mining camp at a

166

gallop.

In front of the community firehouse alongside Slankard & Company's trading-post, Troy flung himself from the stirrups and leaped to throw his weight on the pleated bullhide rope which connected with the clapper of the five-hundred-pound bronze bell in the cupola.

The deafening tintinnabulation of the bell gonged out over the drowned valley, rousing metallic echoes which the steady drumbeat of the storm could not obliterate.

Jodie's face was a pale oval in the murk as Troy grabbed the boy, pulling him from his horse.

"You take the far side of the street, boy. Warn folks in Beagle's Saloon and Slankard's place and on to the courthouse. Tell 'em to get to higher ground. I'll cover the other side."

The clangor of the firebell, rung only in times of desperate emergency, had already brought a rush of men from the doors of saloons and honkytonks along Conconully's main street.

They took up the shout of "Flood! Flood!" and miners sprinted for their private cabins to warn sleeping partners of impending disaster.

Providentially, a rift came in the scudding storm clouds and the wan rays of a sickle moon illumined the town, showed Del Troy the rush of humanity heading for the higher slopes above Salmon Creek.

The Loop-Loop Casino was already emptied by the time Troy drove his horse up the porch steps. He crossed on to Elliott's Hotel and shouted his warning to the crowd congregated under its awning, and left pandemonium in his wake as he raced over the Salmon Creek bridge toward the Cariboo House.

The lobby was already deserted when he got there. Upset tables revealed where a group of late diners had quit the hostelry, running for their lives. The lights burning in Shasta Ives's suite upstairs sent Troy racing up the steps.

The door of room F was partially open, and lamplight revealed a note pinned to the outside panels:

Del: Have been called to Ambie Pride's for midwife duty. Roxanna will tell you why I called you back to town.

Shasta.

Shasta, then, was safe. Pride's shanty was well above the threat of the flash flood. In the act of turning away from the door, Troy's eye was arrested by a seeping puddle of crimson which was pooled under the crack of the door.

He shoved it open, and stood transfixed by what he saw.

Roxanna Laranjo sat against the doorjamb, head on chest. The back of her rain-soaked dress was gorged with congealing blood.

Even as he lifted her, Troy knew that this woman of mystery, his friend and confidante across a span of nearly fifteen years, was beyond his help.

He carried his limp burden into the next room and laid her gently on the candlewick spread of Shasta's four-poster bed. His eye, following a crimson trail across the rug, was led to the open window and the fresh bloodstains which blotched the sill.

Murder had been done in Shasta Ives's room tonight. Not until Troy looked again at Roxanna's placid face, chalk-white in the lamplight shafting through the doorway, did he see the single-shot derringer which the girl clutched in stiffening fingers.

The dead must wait Troy had a duty to the townfolk

who lived farther down the valley. In the act of turning away from the still form on the bed, he remembered something. He bent quickly and snapped the fragile necklace which girdled Roxanna's neck.

He slipped the gold wedding ring into his own pocket, recalling the premonitory words Roxanna had once uttered, her wish that he should have that ring when she was gone. The crucifix he placed in her dead hand, after gently removing the derringer.

"*Hasta luego,* dear one," he whispered, bending to kiss Roxanna's waxen brow. "I'll be back, *querida.* Sleep, sweet—"

He pocketed the derringer as he quit the room, and went on downstairs only after making sure that no guests were asleep in the other hotel rooms.

Farther down the valley, at the south edge of Conconully, lights glowed in homes which would be menaced by the flood when it broke. Troy had barely hit the saddle when a cataclysmic roar of sound burst on his ears and, reining about, he beheld the most soul-sickening spectacle of his life.

With a banshee wail, a solid wall of water rushed down the canyon above Conconully, striking the flats and spreading in a fifteen-foot wall of irresistible doom.

A cloudburst in the upper mountains and intervening log jams along the course of the creek had backed up the lethal waters until, giving way under their cumulative pressure, the flash flood had gathered its full strength.

To save his own life, Troy sent his steelduster rocketing up the pine-clad slope behind the Cariboo House. From that vantage point he saw the tidal wave of debris-littered water strike the firehouse and topple its forty-foot tower. The bell gave out one clanging knell before it was engulfed and shattered.

The log stockade of Slankard's trading-post toppled like cardboard and the corrals and barn and warehouse were wiped out. The Loop-Loop Casino, its windows ablaze, jolted crazily from its foundation and then collapsed askew like a house of cards.

Geysering fountains of spray dashed skyward from the stone barrier of the Silver Exchange Bank, dividing the waters enough to spare Beagle's Saloon the full brunt of their might. Grainger's gun shop floated free of its foundation and whirled past the spot where Troy had gained sanctuary above high-water mark.

Trees uprooted like weeds. Rolling boulders of incalculable mass were driven before the foaming waters like boys' marbles. The full crest of the sprawling flood hit the Cariboo House, caving its flimsy wooden walls, bringing the long roof down like a canopy which floated off like some grotesque ark.

"God bless you, Roxanna."

The flood swept on down the valley. Elliot's Hotel rode the waters briefly, then disappeared. The roof of the stone jail stood like a rock in the face of the flood, debris piling up before its barrier.

In the space of two minutes the waters lessened, their force spent on the open valley, and where Conconully had stood was now a draining, gurgling bowl of mud and rocks and debris, the evidence of human tenure expunged as if by a stroke of a giant broom.

The flash flood was over, the storm retreating into the Cascades. The sucking waters of Salmon Creek sang the swan song of a town that in the space of a hundred seconds had been swept into limbo. Conconully was no more.

CHAPTER TWENTY-THREE

LAST WILL AND TESTAMENT

THE MORROWING SUN FOUND THE POPULACE OF Conconully wandering dazedly over denuded mudflats and mounds of dripping wreckage, searching for vanished possessions, for some scrap of debris they could identify as having marked the site of the vanished boom camp.

Beagle's Saloon loomed gaunt and alone in an area scoured to the bedrock by the passage of the waters. Its barroom was jammed with splintered logs and boulders and flotsam from upcreek mines. By some fantastic caprice of the flood, its costly twenty-foot backbar mirror had not suffered so much as a single fracture, its polished prisms reflecting the ceiling from its place on the caved-in wall.

Del Troy, more mobile than the others because he was on horseback, cruised the length of the gutted valley again and yet again in search of some trace of Roxanna Laranjo's body. But the girl's remains were to rest forever unfound, somewhere under the deep silt of the valley floor. The rocky hillslopes round about would protect her grave through millenniums of time.

Miraculously, Conconully had no other loss of life to mourn as an aftermath of the calamity which had rubbed the county seat and the homes of half a thousand people off the map. This flood would be the date from which future events would be measured; its uneasy past was condemned to oblivion, even as Steen Slankard had predicted in June.

With the exception of Beagle's Saloon, there was

little evidence that a thriving town had stood here yesterday. The stone vaults of the Silver Exchange Bank and a lodge hall remained intact, stark under the sunlight like tombstones needing only epitaphs to become permanent reminders of the camp's existence.

Wherever Del Troy rode, stories of heroism and comedy and pathos reached him. Of how Steen Slankard had risked his life to free the animals trapped in his rock-walled barn; how aging Sheriff Gaddy had unlocked his jail and dragged two drunken inmates to safety, the waters lashing armpit high before he got his charges to the higher ground of the courthouse square.

Troy found Steen Slankard excavating his half-buried safe two hundred yards from the site of his trading post. The thousand-pound vault had been carried like a chip by the rush of waters, and its recovery was little short of a miracle.

But for a man who had lost everything but the clothes on his back, Slankard appeared to be taking his misfortune philosophically.

"I was covered by insurance," he explained to the Texan, as he watched seepage fill the hole where his safe was buried. "Good thing, so far as I was concerned. I aimed to sell out and go back to my lumber mills on the Sound, anyhow."

Troy managed a grin, remembering something Slankard had told him on the eve of the forest fire.

"Didn't you say you'd bought a couple of steamships, Steen? You could have launched 'em in Conconully last night."

Slankard wiped his muddy hands on his beard and fished in a pocket of his butternut jumper, handing Troy a clipping from a recent Seattle *Post-Intelligencer*. It carried a photograph of two deep-sea freighters, tied up at the docks of South Bend.

"Six-thousand tonners," Slankard explained. "The *Nahcotta* and the *Willapa*. Bought 'em sight unseen when a lumber outfit went into receivership down on Shoal-water Bay."

Del Troy returned the clipping with a laugh.

"You'd buy a herd of elephants if you could get 'em at a bargain, you old Shylock," he gibed. "What'll you do with a couple of steamships?"

Slankard leaned on his shovel.

"Aim to cut me a slice of the money that's coming out of Alaska," he said shrewdly. "I've got deep-water docks over on Whatcom Bay. They say lumber fetches its weight in gold dust up at Juneau and Ketchikan. From now on I'll do my own shipping, instead of paying another man half my profits in freight."

Troy moved off, spotting Sheriff Irv Gaddy poking around the puddled rockpile which had been the county jail. From the moment of his discovery of Roxanna's dead body in the Cariboo House, he had decided to confide in no one but the lawman.

Drawing Gaddy out of earshot of a group of men who were grubbing for treasure at the site of the Loop-Loop Casino, Troy recounted his gruesome discovery.

". . . She'd been shot in the back, sheriff," Troy concluded. He drew Roxanna's derringer from his pocket and ejected the fired cartridge from it. "She had this in her hand. I saw blood on the carpet of Shasta's bedroom, leading toward the window sill. Whoever she shot it out with made a getaway just before the flood hit, I figger. Her body was still warm."

Gaddy fingered the star on his suspender strap, shock graven deep on his craggy face. The fact that Roxanna Laranjo was missing was already common knowledge in

173

the town, but she was believed to have been asleep in her room over the Loop-Loop when the Casino was wrecked by the flood.

"I got a message from Shasta, asking me to visit her in the room where Roxanna was killed," he told the sheriff. "I'm trying to figure this thing out. Do you suppose—"

The sheriff cut in, finishing Troy's thought, "You're wondering if Bix Herrod is mixed up in this? I ain't seen that range hog around this morning. Might be we ought to mosey up to Godette's cabin and see if Herrod's accounted for, son."

They waded the brimming width of Salmon Creek and passed the flooded basement of the Cariboo House. The tarpaper shanty which Doc Godette and Herrod had rented after their return from the burned-out cow camp on the Strip was perched on a shelf directly above.

Doc Godette was pumping a bucket of water in front of the shanty when Troy and the sheriff walked up the path. The oldster had his sleeves rolled back, his arms scrubbed septically clean.

"Mornin', gents," the old war dog greeted them. "Quite a calamity last night. I'm lucky I didn't appropriate an empty house on the flats."

The sheriff stared past Godette, into the darkened interior of the cabin. A man lay on the bunk there, the gleam of torn cloths which bandaged his naked midriff visible from where Gaddy was standing.

"Treating a patient this mornin', Doc?"

Godette finished pumping and moved as if to block their view of the cabin door.

"Yeah. Bix Herrod. He was down at the Loop-Loop when the firebell started ringin' last night. A little tipsy, he was, and Herrod can't amble very rapid when he's in

174

his cups. The flood caught him crossin' the bridge and bashed him up considerable. I found him down the hill this mornin', half drowned."

Acting on a sudden hunch, Del Troy shoved past Godette and strode into the shack, halting beside Herrod's bunk. The Lazy H rancher was unconscious. The room was thick with chloroform odors and Godette's surgical instruments were laid out on a split-pole table by the bed, glittering in neat array on a boiled towel.

"You sure Herrod ain't suffering from a gunshot wound, Doc?"

Godette bent a quick stare at Troy as he entered the room, the Conconully sheriff at his heels.

"An unethical question to ask a medical man, *amigo.*"

Troy laughed harshly. "*You* speak of ethics?"

Godette coughed. "*Touché,* my friend. No. I assure you I am treating Bix for lacerations and internal injures sustained in last night's flood. It's too early to tell if he'll rally out of it. I got him under opiates now."

Troy's glance returned to the line-up of scalpels and suture needles, hemostats and forceps on Godette's table. They were the tools a surgeon might employ in probing for a bullet; even a layman could ascertain that.

"Come on, sheriff," Troy said abruptly. "At least we know Herrod didn't drown."

Godette stared after them as the two men headed off down the slope toward the scene of devastation.

"I'd bet my bottom dollar Doc fished Roxanna's bullet out of Bix's hide," Troy muttered. "But that's something we'll never be able to prove."

As they crossed the creek, Shasta Ives approached them on horseback. The girl's face was gaunt from a sleepless night.

175

"A boy or a girl at Ambie's, Shasta?" Troy greeted her, purposely stalling off any reference to the tragedy which had descended on Conconully during her absence.

Shasta's eyes clouded as she drew rein alongside them. "That was a strange thing, Del," she said. "Mrs. Pride isn't expecting her baby for another week at least."

"How," demanded the sheriff, "did you happen to go over to Pride's last night?"

"Ambie came to the Cariboo House to get me, saying Doctor MacAdam had already left and that Jennie needed my help. But it was a false alarm, an outright lie on Ambie's part. The doctor wasn't even there."

Troy and the sheriff exchanged glances. It was obvious that Ambie Pride had maneuvered to get Shasta out of town for some obscure reason.

"We'll ask Ambie why he pulled off that hoax, Miss Ives," the sheriff said. "I got a hunch he was bribed to do it."

Shasta pressed a palm over her eyes.

"I've already seen Ambie. He came home this morning and told us about the flood. The drunken scoundrel can't even remember talking to me last night, he says."

Del Troy fingered his gun butt, his thoughts far away.

"Del, you haven't asked me why I sent for you," she said. "I wanted to tell you that Bix Herrod plans to sell out his Lazy H down in Yakima and buy Flaming Canyon from Okanogan Jones. You've heard the Strip is to go on public sale October first?"

Troy nodded, and gestured off toward Godette's cabin. "I know. Shasta, I've got bad news for you. Your fiancé was hurt last night. Caught in the flood when it

176

washed out the Salmon Creek bridge. Godette's got him up at his cabin yonder."

Shasta's face altered, but her reply did not strike the man as that of a grief-stricken bride-to-be.

"At least he won't be leaving for Yakima to sell his ranch today then." She fixed her eyes on Troy, her thoughts running ahead to other things. "Del, I want to talk to you about selling my cattle to a Seattle shipping company for sale in Alaska. I got a letter offering me sixty dollars a head, after you left town yesterday. That's one reason I sent for you. Roxanna Laranjo has the letter I wanted her to show you. As soon as I find her—"

The averted faces of the two men told Shasta that something was amiss.

"Roxie drowned last night, ma'am," the sheriff said gently. "Del and I been scouting for her body this mornin'. She was the only victim of the flood, so far as we know."

Shasta's cheeks turned ashen, and she swayed slightly in the saddle as she absorbed the tragic news.

"The poor, poor thing. I loved her like a sister." She pulled herself erect and glanced off in the direction of Doc Godette's cabin. "I'll ride over and see how Bix is getting along. Let me know if you—if you locate Roxanna, Del."

After she had gone, Troy turned to the sheriff.

"It all fits, sheriff. Ambie Pride tricked Shasta into leaving the hotel. Herrod was probably back of that deal. Roxie went to see Shasta for some reason or other and found Herrod waiting there to kill me. It fits. It's got to be that way."

Gaddy swore softly under his breath.

"Sure. And we'll never be able to pin it on Herrod."

He spat angrily. "I hope the bastard doesn't pull through. Shasta will be better off if he dies."

An hour later, returning from a third fruitless quest down the valley for some trace of Roxanna's body, Troy was hailed from the county courthouse by Dazzy Kline, the recorder. Riding up to meet him, Troy waited.

"Is it a foregone conclusion that Miss Laranjo is lost?"

"I'm afraid so."

"Then alight and come into my office, Troy. Seeing as how Roxie is officially dead, I've got something she wanted me to give you—in case anything happened to her."

Scowling puzzedly, Troy dismounted and entered the courthouse. Dazzy Kline entered his archives vault and brought out a brown envelope heavy with red seals.

"She left this in my keeping the day after you got back from the fire with Shasta Ives," the recorder said. "Must be her last will an' testament, you reckon?"

Some instinct for privacy sent Troy outdoors, away from Dazzy Kline's inquisitive presence, before he broke open the seals. A document fell out which he saw to be the deed to Keyhole Pass. It was assigned to Del Troy as her beneficiary, and was accompanied by a covering letter, and a bank passbook showing a $7500 balance.

Tears misted Troy's eyes as he read the message, couched in Roxanna's spidery, feminine hand.

Del, querido:

It will perhaps come as a shock to you when I tell you that I have been Bix Herrod's wife for twelve years. We were married at the mission chapel in Villa Acuña in the days when I was a fandango dancer in Del Rio and Bix

178

was running cattle across the Rio Grande.

When the Rangeros forced Bix to come West he left me behind, Del. I followed him to Yakima and not until I learned of his engagement to Shasta Ives did I give up hope of winning back his love.

I came to Conconully to hide myself; I could not bring myself to warn Shasta that she would be entering a bigamous marriage.

Perhaps I shall tell Shasta my secret, one day; I do not know. I do not think Bix loves her; he is incapable of loving any woman.

I will not be alive when you read this. If there should be any element of mystery connected with my death or disappearance, use this information as you see fit.

I think Shasta Ives's heart belongs to you, Del. A woman can tell these things. Think well of me always; I have cherished your friendship.

Vaya con Dios,
Roxie.

P.S. This money is yours, Del. I have no kinfolks.

Del Troy folded the letter and pocketed it. His eyes lifted to the everlasting hills which would forever be the martyred girl's monument, and his mind dwelt at poignant length on her half-revealed saga, knowing that her letter had touched only on the edges of her tragedy.

Roxanna's secret was his legacy, to be kept inviolate from the world, even from Sheriff Gaddy. His glance strayed across the devastated valley and rested briefly on the door of Godette's cabin. Perhaps, at the end, Roxanna had achieved retribution for all she had suffered in her brief span of life.

179

CHAPTER TWENTY-FOUR

GOLDEN BEEF

WAGONS CAME UP FROM RUBY THROUGHOUT THE afternoon, loaded with tentage and food, stoves and bedding—a neighboring community coming to the relief of its stricken sister. By nightfall a tent city had sprung up on the drying sandflats of the town site, and lanterns and torches and blazing tar barrels formed a semblance of ordered pattern under the stars.

Troy toiled on the behalf of refugees he had been instrumental in saving from the flood. Roxanna's death had put a blight on him and her legacy, the half-revealed enigma of her past as Bix Herrod's wife, laid a depression on him which found its surcease only in hard physical work.

He saw Doc Godette buying supplies from a wagon which some enterprising trader had sent up from Ruby, and made a point of buttonholing the medico.

"Bix is awake. He'll pull through, barrin' infection. I give him a month before he's on his feet."

From the front of a long tent which housed a makeshift restaurant on the site of the Loop-Loop Casino, Shasta Ives saw the meeting between Godette and Troy, and when Troy entered the eating-place she followed him to a table and common courtesy demanded that he invite her to dine with him.

"You've had trail-drive experience in Texas," Shasta opened the conversation after they had ordered. "I want you to haze my Dollar stuff from Flaming Canyon to Seattle as soon as possible. I have a guarantee of sixty dollars a head from Alaska Maritime."

He regarded her with a strained reticence.

"Doc says Bix is going to pull through. You won't be moving your herd for three or four weeks yet. By then Herrod could take the job off your hands. I imagine he could use the money."

It was a test question, intended to probe beneath the surface of her mood and reveal where she stood as regarded Herrod. But he was caught off guard by her manner of answering it.

She thrust her left hand across the rough deal table, thus revealing the absence of her engagement ring.

"I returned it to Bix yesterday," she answered his unspoken query. "My decision was a long time in coming, but it was written in the book. Now everything is finished between us."

His thoughts flashed back to the first and only time their lips had met, the morning after the fire which had razed Methow Valley, and wild urges sprang unbidden into his blood.

"I won't say I'm sorry," he temporized. "Herrod was not for you. I've always known that. What do you plan to do now?"

"Ship my cattle to Seattle. With your help. So that you'll have money enough to keep Bix from grabbing all of Flaming Canyon, at least."

Steen Slankard passed their table on his way outside, a quill toothpick waggling from his teeth. The trader nodded to them and headed on toward the door of the tent, then halted as Del Troy called him back.

"Sit down, Steen. I've got a business proposition for you."

Slankard grinned, pulled up a powder-keg chair and sat down. "Always willin' to talk business, my friend. You probably know that better than most."

Troy turned to Shasta Ives, his face lighted with a vitality which had not been there a moment before.

"Shasta, I'm your new trail boss. Which makes me responsible for getting the best possible deal for your cattle, doesn't it?"

She stirred in her chair, catching his eagerness.

"Of course. But I already have a buyer lined up. I—"

Troy's eyes silenced her. Slankard watched on, shrewd lights glinting under his shaggy brows.

"Steen," Troy said, "a Seattle firm is ready to contract to buy Miss Ives's cattle at sixty bucks a head, for butchering and shipment by water to Alaska Would you say she was getting a good proposition?"

The trader fingered his toothpick thoughtfully.

"No. Cattle is at a premium during a drought year. Beef is worth twenty dollars a pound up north. A sixty-dollar cow would fetch three hundred at Skagway."

Troy's eyes lighted triumphantly. He leaned toward the grizzled trader, keeping his voice low.

"You've got two steamships for the Alaska lumber trade on your hands. You've got docks already built on the Sound. I could drive Shasta's herd overland to your gangplank in three weeks. I'm giving you a chance to clean up a fortune, old-timer."

Slankard's eyes, trained in the tricks of his trade, revealed not so much as a spark of interest.

"I'm a lumberman, not a butcher."

Troy brushed Slankard's parry aside, sure of his ground now.

"Look, Steen. I'll push that Dollar herd across the mountains to your docks. You load 'em aboard those two tubs you bought and ship 'em to Alaskan ports. You said yourself you could get three hundred bucks a head from Alaskan buyers. Shasta will sell them to you for a

182

hundred dollars."

Slankard leaned back, laughing. "Hold on, young feller. How'd I feed and water them critters during a week's voyage? I might have a cargo of buzzard bait on my hands if we hit rough weather on the Inland Passage. You got to be practical."

The Texan hurried on, warming to his subject. "Don't ship 'em alive! Butcher 'em at the docks. Salt the beeves down below decks. They'd be easier to stow than lumber."

Slankard shook his head, but he was plainly interested now. "It takes a week, ten days to make the run. Lumber keeps. Fresh-butchered meat would taint in a hot ship's hold."

But Troy's mind had run far ahead of Slankard's objections. "You've seen the glacier fields around Mount Baker, Steen. You could haul enough ice from the mountains to refrigerate your ships, ice that would cost nothing but the hauling. Your lumber mills would furnish the sawdust to keep your ice from melting. You've got tons of salt in your warehouses. You could ship meat clear to China without it spoiling on you."

Steen Slankard thumbed his armpits and teetered back on his powder keg, eyes narrowing as he regarded Shasta. "A hundred bucks a head, delivered at my wharf," he mused. "How big a herd you got?"

Troy supplied that information promptly. "Five fifty, five sixty. Call it an even five hundred. That would net Shasta a gross of fifty thousand dollars. You see"—Troy hesitated—"Shasta aims to move the Dollar from Yakima to Flaming Canyon, Steen, before Bix Herrod buys that graze from Okanogan Jones. We've got barely three weeks to raise the money. It'll take thirty-five thousand to swing the deal with Jones."

Slankard spat out his toothpick and got to his feet.

"I'm beginnin' to see how the wind blows," he grinned. "Didn't smell Bix Herrod in the woodpile. How soon could you get those steers on the trail?"

Slankard had risen to the bait, and from past dealings with the wise old trader Troy knew the bargain was as good as sealed.

"By day after tomorrow," he promised rashly. "You'll need time to get your ships into Puget Sound anyhow. And on the return voyage, you'll more than make expenses bringing cheechakos back from the Klondike at two-fifty a head."

Slankard eyed Shasta Ives with a paternal benevolence. "You planning to tie up with this young scamp on a Flaming Canyon cattle outfit, young lady?"

The truth was there in Shasta's eyes, for all the world to see, and Del Troy took his cue, caught in the dramatic spell of this moment, and blurted out, "Shasta's money will buy Flaming Canyon," he said, "but I go along with the range. As her husband, if she'll take me. As her foreman if she won't."

Slankard settled back on his seat, knowing as he saw this young couple join hands across the table that they were oblivious to his presence. He coughed discreetly and, rummaging in a vest pocket, laid a worn, shiny nickel on the table.

"This is the first nickel I ever earned," he said. "Money is the only religion I got. I don't make deals running into six figgers without being perty sure of garnering myself a profit."

The trader sat closer to the table, worming a bottle of whisky from his jumper pocket, the one thing he had saved from his vanished trading-post. He pulled their coffee cups to him and sloshed out three stiff drinks.

"Here's to fillin' the bellies o' them hongry Klondikers with Dollar beef this winter," he chuckled. "And to your honeymoon in Flaming Canyon. May your hosses never go lame."

CHAPTER TWENTY-FIVE

RACE AGAINST TIME

CONCONULLY, WITH A FAITH IN ITS CONTINUED prosperity as a silver camp, was too engrossed in reconstructing the ruined settlement before the advent of winter to pay any attention to the feverish activity which was transpiring in Flaming Canyon during the days which followed.

Bix Herrod's first intimation that Shasta Ives was making a cattle drive a month ahead of schedule came when the Lazy H rancher, recuperating from his bullet wound in Doc Godette's cabin overlooking the flats, saw the long russet column of Dollar beef moving up the main street, heading west into the mountains.

Unable to leave his bed until his damaged tissues were beyond the danger of internal hemorrhage, Herrod dispatched Doc Godette to investigate. When the oldster returned, he had disturbing news.

"Seems Dollar is headin' across Cascade Pass to salt water, Bix. She's made some kind of a deal with Steen Slankard to ship her beef to Alaska. Accordin' to the drovers, she stands to collect a hundred bucks a head."

Herrod made some rapid computations in his head.

"Fifty thousand dollars," he mused. "Doc, you can see what she's aiming at. Del Troy's talked her into

185

buying Flaming Canyon when Okanogan Jones holds his public sale the first of the month."

Godette, easing a coughing attack with whisky, said nothing.

"Doc, we can copper Troy's bet. You're saddling up today and returning to Yakima. You'll sell out Lazy H at ten cents on the dollar if you have to. I want you back here with at least forty thousand in specie by October first."

Godette eyed his boss narrowly.

"And leave you here to change your dressings and cook your own grub? The only thing you'd need money for would be a coffin."

Herrod swung his feet out of the blankets and stood up. His knees wobbled and he sat down again, cursing his impotence.

"Doc MacAdam can take care of me till you get back. You can close the deal and get back in two weeks."

Godette grunted. "And let the sheriff find out you've got a bullet hole in your hide? Uh-uh."

Herrod stared out the door at the dust of the trail herd smoking the valley.

"I'll tell MacAdam the flood pushed me into a spike and punctured my belly. Saddle and ride, Doc. We can't waste a day."

Godette packed his corncob and got the pipe going. He wore a dubious scowl as he fingered the Yankee saber scar on his cheek.

"Dead sure you know what you're doing? You've spent years building up a spread down there. Don't tear it down without giving it due thought, son."

Herrod cursed until the exertion left him spent and gasping.

"Hell's fire! Flaming Canyon is good the year 'round. No droughts to worry about—this summer proved that. I

186

would never have settled in Yakima if I'd known about the Okanogan."

Doc Godette rode out of Conconully that afternoon, Yakima bound with Herrod's power-of-attorney in his pocket. His patient owed his life to the fact that Roxanna Laranjo's .41 slug had hit a rib and been deflected away from lung tip and liver. With ordinary precautions, Godette knew that Bix Herrod would make a full recovery, thanks to his own surgical genius the night of the flood.

Shasta Ives remained in Conconully, living as a guest at the Ambie Pride home. A week later an incoming stage brought word from Del Troy that the Dollar herd had safely traversed the burn between Twisp and the upper Methow Valley, and was pushing westward through the high gap of Cascade Pass, the first cattle herd in the history of the state to cover that route.

Steen Slankard was conspicuous for his absence in the mining camp, but that occasioned no comment. The word had gone out that Slankard did not intend to rebuild his trading-post; he was quitting the Okanogans in favor of his lumbering interests on the Sound.

What Conconully did not know was that Slankard had two lumber freighters steaming up the Washington Coast, soon to drop their mudhooks in Whatcom Bay.

Del Troy was handicapped by lack of a full crew, but enough of Sam Ives's faithful drovers had rallied to Shasta's call to shove the herd across the mountains.

Ten days out of Conconully saw the vanguard of the herd at the headwaters of the Skagit, picking up tallow on the trail. Averaging ten miles a day, they reached salt water at Slankard's mill on Whatcom Bay on September twenty-eighth, the same morning that the twin steamers *Nahcotta* and *Willapa* anchored in the roadstead after a coaling stop at Port Townsend, across the inlet.

Slankard had done his advance work well. A train of prairie wagons plied day and night between the tide-flats and Mount Baker's glacier fields, hauling block ice for stowage aboard the waiting steamers. Slaughterhouse crews brought up from Seattle were on hand with pole axes and skinning knives, ready to butcher the Dollar steers before Del Troy got the cattle inside Slankard's makeshift pens on the outskirts of his logging camp.

A letter from Shasta, addressed to Troy in Slankard's care, was awaiting the Texan on his arrival;

I have received word from Yakima friends that Bix has sacrificed Lazy H to a local syndicate. That can only mean one thing, Del. Bix will use that money to buy Flaming Canyon from Okanogan Jones, as he told me he planned to do.

October first is just around the corner, and Jones will sell to the first buyer. Can't you telegraph Mr. Slankard's payment to the Silver Exchange Bank here in Conconully, so I can beat Herrod to Jones's land sale?

First and last a businessman, completely devoid of sentiment in his dealings, Steen Slankard was undisposed to pay off until he had personally tallied the Dollar herd. Troy showed him Shasta's letter, with its desperate emphasis on haste.

"The Overland Telegraph lines have been down since the fire, Steen," Del said earnestly. "I'll have to ride day and night as it is to reach Conconully in time to meet Okanogan Jones's deadline for the sale. I'll settle for a flat five hundred head and you can take the excess as your pound of flesh."

That night, September twenty-eighth, Del Troy headed into the Cascades astride his steeldust mustang, figuring that by pushing Alamo to the limit of his endurance he could reach Conconully by early morning of October first. Jones had advertised his sale to start at 9:00 a.m.

He carried with him a bank draft for thirty-five thousand dollars, drawn to Okanogan Jones to facilitate their negotiations; together with Steen Slankard's personal check for the remaining fifteen thousand, payable to Shasta Ives.

At the very hour of his departure from Slankard's mills, an incoming stage brought another letter from Shasta Ives:

Doc Godette got back to Conconully today. I'm positive he turned over the Yakima money to Bix. Please hurry, darling! We can't lose Flaming Canyon at the eleventh hour.

Your own devoted,
Shasta.

P.S. Great news! It's twins at the Ambie Pride household: a six-pound boy named Reid and a seven-pound girl named Lucy. Ambie is so dismayed he's climbed aboard the waterwagon.

Troy made a five-hour stop his first night at a timber cruiser's camp on the Skagit. Dawn of the twenty-ninth found him in saddle and when sunset put his elongated shadow down the old Indian trace he was using as a shortcut, he was midway between Cascade and Twisp Passes, on the lofty rooftree of the mountain range.

He bolted a supper at a telegraph repair crew camp in the shadow of Reynolds Peak, with the serpentine length of Lake Chelan catching the moonglades off to the south, and the cool hours of September's last day paced him down the Twisp wagon road into the burned-out wilderness of the Methow.

He pushed the steelduster until midnight, and made a dry camp near the spot where the charred wreckage of Guff Latchskin's stagecoach lay rusting on the mountain side. Exhaustion claimed both horse and rider, and October's first dawn was in their eyes when they hit the home stretch toward Conconully, twenty miles away across the lowering ridges.

Alamo was maintaining a steady lope down the snag-bordered grade, into the green country untouched by the August holocaust, when the morning hush was breached by the report of a gunshot.

The bullet's close passage was an airwhip on Troy's earlobe, and instinct sent him diving from saddle into a fernbrake hedge bordering the road, his Colt .45 palmed before he hit the ground.

Every nerve of his body was keyed to a wire-taut pitch as he cuffed off his Stetson and burrowed deeper into the underbrush. A spiral of gunsmoke located his ambusher as lurking in the concealment of an eroded heap of towering glacial boulders, on the opposite side of the road and down the grade a few yards.

Troy waited, gun cocked, hoping against hope that the bushwhacker would not shoot his mustang, halted in the open road. He was primed to shoot the instant his attacker ventured out of the rock nest to investigate.

Suddenly there came to Troy's ears the muffled sounds of a raucous, spongy cough, the hard spasms of a consumptive wracking his lungs.

Troy's mouth twisted in a grin of recognition as he gained the shelter of a spruce bole to get the sun's strike out of his eyes. He thumbed a shot toward the boulders and called out in a bantering voice, "Show yourself, Doc."

The coughing finally subsided, to be followed by a weighty silence. Somewhere far off a woodpecker drilled at a dead snag; the wind was a soughing melody through the conifers overhead.

"Reckon I'll hang and rattle, Troy," a voice reached him from the boulder pile. "It's cool and safe in here."

Time was running out fast for the Texan. Okanogan Jones was due in Conconully this morning, to open his land sale. Minutes were precious, yet Troy knew it would be suicidal to come into the open and attempt running Godette's ambuscade.

A curl of tobacco smoke from the medico's ubiquitous corncob drifted up from a cleft between two rocky pinnacles, betraying Godette's approximate location. Troy aimed at the sloping brow of rock and drove a shot in from an angle, heard the bullet ricochet with the scream of a plucked harpstring as it smeared off the granite.

There was a sound of creaking saddle leather behind the rocks and a moment later the scrawny figure of Doc Godette appeared, mounted on his line-back grulla. The oldster had his arms up, his ancient Spiller and Burr revolver dangling by the trigger guard from his right thumb.

The bloody track of a bullet had joined the puckered saber scar on Godette's hollow cheek.

"Won't swap words or lead with a man who carroms a billiard shot around corners at me," Godette chuckled, halting his horse in mid-road. "I'm your meat, son."

Troy recovered his sombrero and stepped out into the open, wary and alert for treachery, his Colt covering the old-timer.

"Heave that blunderbuss over here, Doc. And you bragging you could knock out a bluejay's eye at fifty paces—"

Godette regarded his rusty percussion pistol wistfully, then tossed it in the dust at the Texan's feet.

"I carried that iron at Vicksburg an' Kennesaw Mountain an' the first battle o' Bull Run under Beauregard," he reminisced. "Hate to lose it."

Troy picked up the Spiller and Burr, removed the priming caps and flung the Confederate weapon as far as he could into the trees.

"Make your first shot count, son," Godette begged. He tapped his chest. "Figger I only got a month or two left anyhow. This way is better. I been livin' on borrowed time for quite a spell."

Troy walked over to his steelduster and mounted, holstering his own gun. He eyed Doc Godette indifferently. "Herrod post you here to hold me off?"

Godette's eyes were evasive. "I was born on a key off the Gulf coast," he commented irrelevantly. "Ain't seen salt water since. I was headin' toward the Sound. When I seen you I figgered you had Shasta's beef money on you. Thought I'd soak my feet in tidewater and have myself one hell of a last fling."

Troy spurred on past the old man.

"Salt water lies a hundred and fifty miles yonderward," he said. "Hit the trail, Doc."

Godette picked up his reins, a rare twinge of conscience laying its sharp edge against him. When Troy was fifty feet beyond him, the old medico wheeled his mount and called out.

"Troy! You should know Bix Herrod's up and around this mornin'. With forty thousand in specie to offer Okanogan Jones. You'll have to hurry. I wish you luck."

Troy made no answer.

"He'll be tough to buck in a shoot-out, son. Roxie tried at point-blank range and failed. The man's bullet-proof."

Godette had cut his last tie of allegiance with the partner of his last twenty years, but he felt no remorse, no sense of treachery. He owed Herrod nothing, in the last analysis, not even the coin of loyalty.

"Thanks, Doc," Troy said evenly. "I thought that was the way it was. I'll even Roxie's score for her. *Adios.*"

When the beat of the steelduster's hoofs had died beyond the ridge, Godette felt a new spasm rising in his lungs and he hastily searched his kitbag for a shot of whisky to stall off the pain. The bottle was empty, and in the amber glass Godette seemed to read an augury of his own expiring powers.

He got off the horse as the first paroxysms came, and stripped the grulla of its saddle and bridle. Then he seated himself against a hemlock sapling at the roadside and hugged his knees in his arms, his head bent forward.

Godette was frozen in that rigid posture two days later when a passing mines paused to stare at the grulla saddle horse which stood faithful to its last lone vigil there.

CHAPTER TWENTY-SIX

CROWNING HOUR

OKANOGAN JONES DROVE INTO CONCONULLY AT NINE o'clock sharp with his blanket-draped squaw riding the box of his democrat wagon. The oldster turned his rig into the shade of Beagle's Saloon and hitched his mules to a tree which stood at an angle to the ground, half uprooted by the flood's passage.

The erstwhile king of the Twenty-Mile Strip unrolled a sheet of canvas and tacked it to the clapboards of the saloon wall. It bore a crude legend brushed on with tar: *Public Land Sale Here Now.*

From the porch of Doc Godette's shanty overlooking the tent-dotted town, Bix Herrod noted the squaw man's arrival and went into the cabin to make preparations for his first trip into town.

Donning his fustian coat, the rancher buckled on his heavy Colt harness. But the drag of the cross-draw guns put agony on strained tissues, and he elected to discard them.

From a go-easter bag on a shelf he took a pair of derringers fitted with spring-clip holsters which, worn high on the wrists, would be concealed by his coat cuffs. It was a rig Herrod had not worn since his Texas days, but instinct warned him not to venture out unheeled.

A meeting with Del Troy did not enter into his calculations, for he had taken care of that contingency. Somewhere out in the hills, Doc Godette had been camped since yesterday, on the off chance that Troy might be trying to beat Okanogan Jones's deadline, this morning. Troy would never pass Doc Godette alive.

The derringers installed, the Lazy H boss turned back his bunk mattress and took out a fat envelope. The envelope contained an even four hundred crisp new hundred-dollar bills, representing the sacrifice sale of his Yakima cattle empire.

Pocketing the currency, Herrod donned his Keevil hat and studied his reflection briefly in a cracked mirror by the door. The face which stared back at him bore the print of his recent suffering, sharpening the line of his jaw and accentuating the predatory cast of his mouth. But his hands were rock steady and new strength flowed through his iron frame, and he knew he was fit.

Emerging into the mellow autumn sunshine, Herrod picked his careful and deliberate way down the path to the temporary footbridge across Salmon Creek.

He was nearing the main street when he sighted Shasta Ives riding into town from the direction of Ambie Pride's place, a shopping-bag looped over her saddle horn.

Herrod saw the girl dismount in front of Moore, Ish & Company's tent mercantile store. She saw him as he approached and said impersonally, "I'm glad you're up and around again, Bix."

"Is that all you have to say to me, Shasta?"

She shrugged, untying her shopping-bag.

"What else is there to say between us?"

He moved toward her, all his old jealousies and stormy pride and injured vanity showing in his tired eyes. "I'm buying Flaming Canyon this morning, Shasta. My offer is still open. It's not too late to share in Lazy H's new deal."

A momentary panic crossed the girl's eyes, and then she looked past him, toward the lather-flecked steeldust mustang which was hitched to the carpenters' scaffold alongside Beagle's Saloon. The fear left her eyes then, and Bix Herrod turned to follow the line of her gaze.

"First come, first served, Jones said," she remarked. "That's Del Troy's horse. You're too late, Bix."

A panic touched Herrod then, and he lurched past her, crossing the street at a limping run, without regard for the cramps in his half-healed muscles.

Shasta started after him with a low cry, only to be brought up short by Sheriff Irv Gaddy, who had stepped from the store tent behind her.

"Stop him, sheriff!" the girl pleaded. "Del's in there. Bix will kill him."

Gaddy shook his head, holding her elbow in a vise-like grip. "No. Bix ain't heeled, and Troy wouldn't take advantage of that. They have got to meet sometime, girl. The worst Troy can hand Herrod is a thrashin' like he gave Whitey Crade."

Bix-Herrod slogged up the saloon steps and shouldered through the slatted half-doors into the barroom. His glance came immediately to rest on Okanogan Jones, who was seated at a poker table nearest the door. In the background, Jones's squaw, Tenas Josie, squatted on the floor, a plat of the Twenty-Mile Strip spread open on her lap.

Jones was alone, scribbling on a sheaf of papers. Herrod approached the table, relief surging through him. "Open for business, Okanogan?"

Jones cocked a hostile eye at the cattleman.

"Anybody fool enough to pay a dollar an acre for my burned-out land, I'll do business with!" the squawman grunted. "Look over Josie's plat and name your wants."

Herrod thumped his sheaf of greenbacks on the baize. "Forty thousand chips in that bundle, Jones. I want the fifty-five sections comprising Flaming Canyon for that money."

Okanogan Jones eyed the money hungrily, then pushed it back. "No dice. Flaming Canyon was sold two minutes ago, Herrod."

Herrod's jaw petrified. "Who bought it?"

Jones jerked a thumb toward the bar, and his hand went to his parfleche jacket in search of his eye glasses.

Herrod wheeled slowly to face the bar. Del Troy stood there with a bottle of whisky and a shot glass before him, one dusty boot hooked over the brass rail. The stamp of a long and grueling trail was on his clothes, rutted deep in his haggard face, but his spiking gaze held the Lazy H boss rooted to his tracks.

"Step over here, Bix. I've got something to show you."

The Lazy H rancher stood like a graven image. This moment had to come, this meeting; it was in the cards. It galled Herrod to know that destiny had switched their fortunes at the time when this meeting had to be, but he found himself stumbling forward, pulled by Troy's voice against his will. A slow fear cramped his stomach, his feet dragged, scraping the boards with a wooden sound.

"I'm not armed, Troy," Herrod cawed. "I'm not ready."

Troy turned to Beagle. "Another glass, please. We're going to drink to Bix Herrod stretching a hang-rope before the year is out. For a murder he doesn't know I'm wise to."

The perspiring bartender skidded a glass down the mahogany, his face ashen. Del Troy reached for the glass, tilting his bottle to decant a dram of amber whisky for his guest.

"I'm not armed—"

Even as Herrod parroted the words, his right hand made a flicking motion and a .41 hide-out gun appeared magically there, from its spring clip under his cuff.

"You had something to show me?" Herrod mocked, insane lights kindling in his eyes as he cocked the derringer.

Del Troy carefully replaced glass and bottle, his face taut. "Before you pull that trigger, Bix, I've got a little keepsake for you. Something you never should have lost. You'll want to know how I got it. It belonged to your wife."

Troy reached for his shirt pocket as he spoke. From the pocket he drew a plain gold ring which shimmered in the light from the backbar glass.

He dropped the wedding ring on the sawdusted floor puncheons at Herrod's feet, drawing the man's eyes with it.

"Roxanna's ring, Herrod. I took it from her dead body the night of the flood. You killed her."

Herrod stared at the golden circlet on the floor, unable to tear his eyes away from it. And in that frozen instant that his foe's attention was off his gun, Del Troy bunched his muscles and brought a chap-clad leg up to smash Herrod's arm.

The Lazy H boss staggered back, bellowing with pain, and Del Troy's out-swiping hand battered the derringer from Herrod's grasp and sent it bouncing across the room.

Herrod made a frantic reach for the bar to break his fall and knocked the whisky bottle to the floor. He saw Troy's bunched fist coming, but was powerless to roll away from the blow.

The punch connected with Herrod's cheekbone in a meaty, sodden impact like a sledge hitting a steer. Herrod reeled back and recovered his balance, seeing the glint of following gun metal as Del Troy made his draw.

Herrod brought his reserve derringer from his left sleeve with all his old-time skill, before Troy's .45 came to a level. The weapons blazed as one, their concussion shaking the overhead lamps into penduluming arcs.

Through smudging gunsmoke, the frozen onlookers saw Herrod's shot pluck a puff of dust from Troy's sleeve and drill its sightless path through space to smash a window light in the back of the barroom with a splintered, chiming crash.

But Troy's aim had been precise, dead center to the bridge of Herrod's nose.

Dead on his feet, the big Lazy H rancher pitched sideways to thump his temple against the curved rim of the bar. His weight pulled him down to the brass rail, one leg out-thrust, the other doubled under him. Then his head sagged back to pillow itself in a tarnished cuspidor that caught his spilling lifeblood.

"For you, Roxie," Troy whispered to the ghost he felt at his side, and stooped to recover the Spanish girl's ring.

Herrod's Hussar boot drummed the floor in brief tattoo, and then the reflexes left his settling hulk and he lay in broken, slack finality alongside the counter, smoke wisping from his derringer bore and eddying milkily in a pull of air currents sucking through the batwings.

Tenas Josie was crooning some ancient tribal death chant in her guttural jargon, over in the corner. The whisky bottle still rolled around the floor in rhythm to her keening melody, a fact which seemed somehow important to Del Troy in that moment, clocking as it did the brief span of time since death had brushed him with its black wings.

Troy stared for an interval at the smoking gun in his hand before replacing it in leather. The street door fanned open and Sheriff Irv Gaddy stepped inside, his eyes summing up the picture before him and finding it to his liking.

"She's across the street, Del," the lawman said, and bent to cover Bix Herrod's blood-gouting face with the Keevil hat. "No use her seeing all this."

199

Del Troy's hand touched the hip pocket of his Levis then, confirming the reality of the bill of sale to Flaming Canyon which Okanogan Jones had signed and delivered a moment before Herrod's arrival. That paper marked the sum total of all his life's strivings, the net result of many spins of the wheel of fate.

Vagrant pictures flashed across the kaleidoscope of his brain, reminding him of the cost of blood and effort that lay behind this crowning hour of his life; and ghosts stalked out of the gunsmoke, demanding their turns in his memory.

He thought of Fred Bolte's scattered bones, bleaching on the cauterized brink of the Dry Falls, and of Whitey Crade's treachery and its grisly price. Fire and flood had joined to delay this moment; Roxanna Laranjo had sacrificed herself in the flower of her womanhood to help bring it about.

And then the reverie faded, and Troy gave Bix Herrod a last searching look, and realized then that he had come to the end of a long black tunnel, that its threats and its hazards were forever behind him.

He stepped around the dead man and through the doorway, squinting against the bright glare of the October sun that touched the mica particles in the dust of Conconully's thoroughfare and turned them to diamond points.

All the tension seemed to pass from him as he descended the saloon steps, walking out to meet Shasta Ives, as the girl he loved ran toward him across the street. He knew then that this was his ultimate prize, the true fulfillment of all that had led them to this meeting.

No words passed between these two—her hands came up to pull his head down with a gentle urgency, and he bent to taste the full rich promise of her betrothal kiss.

We hope that you enjoyed reading this
Sagebrush Large Print Western.
If you would like to read more Sagebrush titles,
ask your librarian or contact the Publishers:

United States and Canada

Thomas T. Beeler, *Publisher*
Post Office Box 659
Hampton Falls, New Hampshire 03844-0659
(800) 251-8726

United Kingdom, Eire, and
the Republic of South Africa

Isis Publishing Ltd
7 Centremead
Osney Mead
Oxford OX2 0ES England
(01865) 250333

Australia and New Zealand

Australian Large Print Audio & Video P/L
17 Mohr Street
Tullamarine, Victoria, 3043, Australia
1 800 335 364